Sutton pulled her and her son up off the couch with ease.

"Thank you." She looked into his eyes, intensely blue and glittering with an emotion she couldn't identify. Whatever it was, it made her feel warm and tingly and a little strange.

Lovely strange. Attracted strange.

Which wasn't good.

Lowrie tightened her grip on her son, forced a polite smile and murmured an "excuse me." She walked past him, cursing herself for feeling disappointed. He might be her only guest right now, but he was still a guest and distance should be maintained.

No, physical and emotional distance *had* to be maintained.

Men—as well as her mother—had used her heart before and she'd never let that happen again.

* * *

The Secret Heir Returns by Joss Wood is part of the Dynasties: DNA Dilemma series.

Will the results of one DNA test upend everything for this American blue blood family?
Don't miss a single twist or turn!

Secrets of a Bad Reputation
Wrong Brother, Right Kiss
Lost and Found Heir
The Secret Heir Returns

Dear Reader,

We're back in Portland, Maine, and this is the last book in the Dynasties: DNA Dilemma series. It's been a real treat to write this series!

On his birthday, London-based author Sutton Marchant discovers he is related to the famous Ryder-White family and is the heir to a massive fortune, but only if he spends two months at the Rossi Inn and attends the famous Ryder International Charity Ball. Sutton is not interested in connecting with his biological family, but the huge fortune is hard to ignore.

Single mom and innkeeper Lowrie Lewis is ecstatic when the famous author books the entire inn to maintain his privacy. A once hugely successful artist, Lowrie is content with her job running the inn and being a mother to her toddler, Rhan. She is flummoxed by her attraction to the secretive Sutton—how did this happen? But Sutton is irresistible and he's soon turning her life upside down.

Keep turning the pages to find out the results of those pesky DNA test results that set off the chain of events that led to my Ryder-Whites finding their happy-ever-afters!

Happy reading!

Joss

Connect with me on:

Facebook: JossWoodAuthor
Instagram: JossWoodBooks
Twitter: JossWoodBooks
BookBub: joss-wood
www.JossWoodBooks.com

JOSS WOOD

THE SECRET HEIR RETURNS

DESIRE™

ISBN-13: 978-1-335-73565-2

The Secret Heir Returns

Copyright © 2022 by Joss Wood

For questions and comments about the quality of this book, please contact us at CustomerService@Harlequin.com.

Harlequin Enterprises ULC
22 Adelaide St. West, 41st Floor
Toronto, Ontario M5H 4E3, Canada
www.Harlequin.com

Printed in U.S.A.

Recycling programs for this product may not exist in your area.

PLEASE RECYCLE · THIS PRODUCT IS RECYCLABLE

Joss Wood loves books, coffee and traveling—especially to the wild places of southern Africa and, well, anywhere. She's a wife and a mom to two young adults. She's also a slave to two cats and a dog the size of a small cow. After a career in local economic development and business, Joss writes full-time from her home in KwaZulu-Natal, South Africa.

Books by Joss Wood

Harlequin Desire

Dynasties: DNA Dilemma

Secrets of a Bad Reputation
Wrong Brother, Right Kiss
Lost and Found Heir
The Secret Heir Returns

Murphy International

One Little Indiscretion
Temptation at His Door
Back in His Ex's Bed

Harlequin Presents

South Africa's Scandalous Billionaires

How to Undo the Proud Billionaire
How to Win the Wild Billionaire

Visit her Author Profile page at Harlequin.com, or josswoodbooks.com, for more titles.

You can also find Joss Wood on Facebook, along with other Harlequin Desire authors, at Facebook.com/harlequindesireauthors!

Prologue

Sutton Marchant shook the hand of the older of the two nattily dressed lawyers and caught the sneer of the younger one. Probably due to Sutton's ratty sweatshirt, battered Levi's and coffee-cup-and-paper-covered desk. He'd pulled an all-nighter working on edits. Feeling sleep-deprived and rough, he wanted to go to bed and sleep for three days, but, apparently, this meeting was urgent and *could not wait*.

Irritated, Sutton led the lawyers over to the sitting area of his study and gestured them to the love seat. He lifted a box filled with copies of his latest release from a chair, put it down on his hardwood floor and sat down, rubbing a hand over his face.

What the hell could be so important? It couldn't be anything to do with work, since his agent and publishers, thank God, dealt with the legalities. And Sam, his business partner, best friend and brother-in-law, was the CEO of MarchBent, their stocks, shares and crypto trading company. If this meeting had anything to do with MarchBent, Sam would be their first port of call. So…what?

Best way to find out was to ask them. "How can I help you?"

The younger lawyer removed a folder from his briefcase and laid it on the coffee table in front of Sutton. He glanced down at it and lifted his eyebrows. The older man leaned back, undid the button of his black suit jacket, hitched his pants leg and crossed one leg over the other.

"As I said, I am Tom Gerard, senior partner at Gerard and Pinkler. This is Albert Cummings, one of our associates. We represent the Tate-Handler Adoption Agency."

Sutton sat up straighter, his heart beating faster. The last time he'd interacted with people from the Tate-Handler Adoption Agency had been seventeen or so years ago, when he and his adoptive parents met with an agency representative. He remembered being handed a brown envelope, and told it contained a letter from his birth mother. He'd coldly, calmly told the representative that he had no interest in who she was or what she had to say.

At eighteen he'd been of the mindset that since she

hadn't wanted him then, he didn't want, or need, her now. And nothing had changed his mind.

"I'm not interested in connecting with my birth mother," Sutton told them, his tone cool.

"So you know who she is?" Gerard asked.

He thought of the unopened brown envelope locked in the small safe behind the painting above his head. "I've never wanted to know. I still don't want to know anything about the circumstances of my birth."

They exchanged a worried glance. "Well, that's a bit of a problem because we're here to tell you that you are the beneficiary of a trust set up by your biological father. As the beneficiary, you own a share in a large company and the control of the trust will pass to you on your thirty-fifth birthday. I believe that is in a day or two?"

Sutton nodded. He rubbed his face with his hands again, trying to force blood into his brain.

"I'm his heir? There are assets?" Sutton looked at the shelf above his desk, where copies of his books were displayed. He was a bestselling author, and the co-owner of a ridiculously successful trading company. He and his sister had inherited millions from their wealthy parents—his father was an internationally renowned economist, his mother a horticulturist—and both were minor branches, twigs really, of England's royal family tree. He and Thea co-owned Marchant House in Sussex, a sprawling estate that had been in the family for over three hundred years that they'd turned into a country hotel.

Basically, he and Thea weren't hurting for money. He did not need anything from his biological father.

"I'm not interested," Sutton told them, leaning back and folding his arms. He'd had parents, and they could never be replaced, by anybody, *ever*. "You can tell him that he can make someone else his heir and beneficiary."

Cummings winced. "It's not that easy, Mr. Marchant. He died shortly after your birth. We have been managing the trust for the past thirty-five years."

Was he supposed to feel sad that a man he never knew had died over three decades ago? Sutton shrugged. He'd mourned his parents for years and years. He didn't have any grief left over for a man he never knew.

"It's not my problem," Sutton said. "I never asked for the inheritance and I don't want it. Give it to his other relatives."

"He left instructions that the trust could not pass to his immediate family."

"Then give it to his wife, lover, friend!"

Gerard shook his head. "That can't happen, either. The person he was in a relationship with when he died passed away a few years ago."

"I. Don't. Want. It." Sutton gripped the bridge of his nose.

"I'm sorry to hear that," Gerard said on a sigh. "But the only way for you to disperse of the trust is to take control of it. Once it's under your control, you can liquidate the assets and do with it whatever you wish. You could, for instance, donate all the proceeds to a charity."

Okay, that was a plan. Sutton placed his ankle on

his knee and linked his hands across his stomach. "Great. Draw up the papers and I will sign whatever you need for that to happen."

Sutton glanced at his watch. Mrs. K, his housekeeper—and the woman who'd been his parents' housekeeper for years before they died—would've already made fresh coffee and would, if he asked her nicely, rustle up an English breakfast. Then he'd hit the sack for a solid eight. This afternoon, he'd go for a run and then have dinner with Adriana, an old flame who dropped in and out of his life.

Since he was allergic to commitment—thanks to his parents' early deaths, he was terrified of someone he loved leaving him—an occasional night of fun suited him just fine.

"Your father—"

"My father and mother died in a car accident, five years ago," Sutton interrupted Gerard, his voice cold.

"Your birth father wanted you to know that he didn't know of your adoption until after the fact. Because of the arrangements your birth mother made with the Tate-Handler Agency, he could not ascertain your identity. He chased down every legal option to get access to you. Obviously, he never succeeded."

Obviously. Sutton squirmed in his chair, feeling guilty that he was even having this conversation. Even discussing the circumstances of his birth made him feel disloyal to his parents.

Gerard continued, "Once you take control of the trust, you can do whatever you want with its assets but—"

Ah, here came the catch. Sutton braced himself.

"—but you can only do that after you spend two consecutive months in Portland, Maine, at a specific inn and attend the annual Ryder International Valentine's Ball."

What? Was he serious?

"If you meet those requirements, you can sell the shares to anyone but your benefactor's brother and disperse his wealth however you see fit. If you choose not to temporarily relocate to Portland for two months, then you cannot do anything with the trust for another fifteen years."

"Wait, let me make sure I understand this correctly—I live in Portland for two months and attend a ball? After that, I can do what I want with the trust? That's…nuts."

"Well, you have to stay at The Rossi Inn for those two months, but yes, that's it."

They both nodded, their faces solemn. Sutton sat up and leaned his forearms on his thighs, dangling his hands between his knees. "He doesn't say anything about me acknowledging him as my birth dad?"

"No," Gerard confirmed, "the will says nothing about you disclosing that he is your father. But you should be aware that there are people looking to discover who owns the shares in the company."

"Why?" Sutton asked.

"The trust owns a twenty-five-percent stake in a multinational, family-run company. Your biological father's brother owns twenty-seven percent, and the rest is owned by shareholders. The brother has wanted to buy your father's shares for the last thirty-five years, but we could not sell to him, or to anybody else. Your biological uncle has been pressuring us for years to disclose the owner but since it's a confidential trust, we cannot, and will not, disclose your identity."

"And I can't sell to him, even if I wanted to?"

Gerard shook his head. "They had a falling-out, and your father's will states you cannot sell to your uncle or any of his descendants."

Family drama—he'd had enough of it in his teens and early twenties. He didn't need it from people he didn't know.

"Look, whether it's now or in fifteen years, you are going to discover who he is. However, if you choose to remain silent about your parentage, you can. You will always be in control of that narrative," Gerard added.

That was something, at least. His mind spinning, Sutton wondered how much money they were talking about. It might be, if he was lucky, a couple of million. Frankly, his parents' charitable foundation would be happy for *any* additional funds. Looking after vulnerable kids was damned expensive.

"What is his estate worth?"

"Close to a hundred and fifty million."

Holy crap.

He saw the gleam in their eyes, their belief the money was getting to him. It was, but not in the way they thought. His parents were crazy-ass philanthropists and their foundation was running a little dry. He, Thea, and Sam, his best friend, tossed money into it as often as they could, but thanks to the COVID-19 pandemic, the well was running low. If he liquidated the trust, the foundation would be flush for the rest of his life. He couldn't think of a better way to spend his birth father's money than to support the causes his parents had been passionate about.

He could work remotely and didn't have a lover keeping him in London—spending two months across the pond and attending a ball wouldn't be a problem. He just hoped the inn was comfortable. But for a hundred and fifty mil, he'd sleep in a tent.

Sutton scratched his head and looked at the folder on the table. "I presume all the documentation is in there?" After they nodded, he spoke again. "I will discover the identity of my birth father by opening that folder. Will I be forced to find out who my birth mother is, too?"

Gerard shook his head. "No, there is nothing in that folder about your birth mother."

Ah, good. He still had no interest in her. As an adult, he hadn't wanted to exchange his adoptive parents for anyone, anywhere, so what was the point of finding out who she was or why she'd done what she had?

Realizing that the trust was now his problem—or would be in the near future—Sutton reached for the folder and flipped it open.

I, Benjamin James Ryder-White, a resident of the State of Maine, Cumberland County, declare that this is my will and testament of my wishes.

One

Portland, Maine

He was here…

Lowrie Lewis parked her ten-year-old sedan next to a very expensive SUV and switched off the engine. She wasn't sure what she'd done to deserve having only one guest to look after for the next two months, but she wouldn't question her good luck. One breakfast, one set of linens changed, laundry for one person…bliss. And the fact that the Englishman had paid a stupendous amount of money to ensure that he had the inn to himself made her want to do a happy dance. The inn was always quiet in the dead of winter but he'd paid her the equivalent rate of having full-to-bursting occupancy, something that never happened this time of the year.

Because he'd paid his enormous bill up front, she could renovate the bathrooms, replace some linens, give some of the guest rooms a fresh lick of paint.

Lowrie looked over her shoulder and saw that Rhan, her one-year-old, had fallen asleep during their short trip back from the store. Mr. Marchant was earlier than expected, she thought, grimacing. She'd wanted to be here to meet him, to give him a tour of The Rossi. Paddy, bless him, would've just handed him the key and waved him up the stairs.

Her great-uncle Carlo, the original owner of this inn, had been a much better host than the irascible Paddy. He'd been hospitality personified. Carlo would've arranged for coffee and cake, placed a rose in a small vase on the tray and gotten Sutton Marchant's life story within a half hour of meeting the author.

She wasn't overly chatty, but from working here in her teens, and then again when she returned from New York after her life fell apart and before she went traveling, she knew how to make a guest feel welcome. Paddy, who'd inherited life rights to the house from Carlo, did not.

Lowrie looked up at the three-story inn, smiling at the soft lavender color. She loved this whimsical house, perched on the edge of a small cliff. Below the house, the stormy winter waters of Casco Bay pounded the rocks and icy waves slapped the tiny beach they used in summer. The house had wraparound verandas on the bottom level and three of the rooms, including the biggest—now the domain of their guest—had substantial balconies. Black shutters provided the perfect contrast to the lavender, and in summer, the garden was vibrant with color.

The interior was as wonderful as the outside, containing comfortable furniture, amazing art and collectibles. It was a place that begged you to relax, to enjoy the views of the sea and the forest.

She loved it here. It was home.

But it was also her workplace and she had lots to do. Exiting the car, she slammed her door shut and glanced up as she did so. A man, dressed in dark blue jeans and a thick, hooded sweatshirt under a sleeveless parka, walked onto the veranda and over to the snow-covered railing. He jammed his hands into the pockets of his parka, and she examined his profile, trying to ignore her rapidly beating heart and suddenly dry mouth.

Masculine was the first word that popped into her head. Followed by *sexy*. He looked to be in his midthirties and was tall, perhaps six-two or six-three, with wide shoulders, longs legs and big arms. In profile, she could see his long nose and brownish, messy hair. His stubborn chin and strong jaw were covered with a couple of days' worth of stubble.

Ripped, built, hot…

He also looked…intelligent, Lowrie decided. But also a little lost, a smidgen sad. And she wanted to know why.

Lowrie shook her head, dropped her gaze and

opened the back door to her car. She undid the buckles holding Rhan in his car seat and lifted her baby up and onto her chest. Sutton Marchant was a guest, and she wasn't looking for a man, any man.

She had her son, a job she loved, her grandmother and aunt down the road. The irascible Paddy. It had been a year since Rex had left her, six since she'd left New York, and her mother and her then fiancé, behind. Her heart was still healing from the pain all those situations had inflicted.

She didn't know if she ever would be open to risking her heart again. It had been trampled on by many people, in different ways and too often for her to take that chance.

Marchant was just another guest and she'd treat him like one.

He should kill Maribeth. Look, he liked her, she was fun and lovely, but she'd outlived her usefulness and it was time for her to go...

Sutton Marchant blinked when fingers snapped in front of his face. He blinked again and slowly the lovely face of his sister, who was also his personal assistant, came into focus. The character Maribeth looked a lot like Thea, he thought. Long blond hair, green eyes, petite and slim. Unlike Thea, Maribeth was a free spirit. Maybe he'd keep her around for another chapter or two. Maybe she could be the one to—

Thea pinched him. Sutton yelped and sent her a ferocious scowl. "I hate it when you do that," he muttered, rubbing the back of his hand.

"I hate it when you zone out on me when I'm talking to you," Thea shot back. Sutton leaned back in his chair and placed his feet on the corner of his new desk, crossing his size thirteens. Thea, efficient as always, was perched on the edge of her seat opposite him, skimming through her iPad.

Sutton looked around his new workspace, which was attached to his expansive bedroom, squinting at the mess through one eye. There were at least four unpacked boxes—containing his can't-live-without-them books, notepads, reference materials, three dictionaries and two thesauruses—and he wished he could click his fingers and have them spring onto the empty shelves of the small bookcase behind the desk.

Or that Thea would stay another few days and do it for him. But she needed to get back to her family in London. He'd told her he could fly to the States and book himself into the inn, but she'd insisted on accompanying him and they'd spent last night in New York City, eating at her favorite restaurant before flying into Portland, Maine, this morning. He'd rented a Jaguar F-Pace and easily found The Rossi Inn, happy to discover that his temporary housing was a very pretty, luxurious inn right on the edge of Maine's rugged coastline, not that far from Portland's city center.

He'd booked the inn for two months, as per the will, but Thea had negotiated with the owner of the property not to take any reservations while he was in residence and compensated them for the lost revenue.

He had complete privacy and run of the historic place. He wasn't George Clooney famous but he was recognized often enough to make him feel uncomfortable.

"As I was saying, they will serve you breakfast, it's included in the rate, but if you want lunch and dinner you have to arrange it with them. Ahead of time, Sutt, not when you are hungry."

"That's why God invented takeout."

Thea shuddered. "You cannot live on takeout alone. You need vegetables. And fruit."

"Wine is made from grapes and that's fruit," he said, purely to wind up his sister, who insisted upon fresh and organic food.

"Shut up," she told him, standing. She looked around the suite and nodded. "Your laptop is set up, so is your printer and you're connected to the Wi-Fi."

Excellent. As soon as she left, he'd plop himself down at the desk in front of the massive window and get to work. Though he might have to face the wall because the 180-degree view of the rocks, beach and sea, just down the dune, was hella distracting.

But, man, he was looking forward to running along this desolate coastline.

"You have a video chat scheduled with your editor tomorrow at three," Thea told him, looking down at her tablet. Thea was a great personal assistant. She was a perfect pain in his ass but she kept him on track. She maintained his website, his mailing lists and kept his social-media posts up-to-date. She scheduled his appearances at bookstores, conventions and fairs, arranged his speaking engagements and, generally, kept his life on track.

She was the barrier between him and the rest of the world.

"I'll send you a text message to remind you." She tapped the edge of her tablet, her expression worried. "It isn't too late to change your mind and just come back to London, Sutt," Thea told him. "This isn't New York or LA, cities you know well."

Oh, and she also thought he couldn't find his way out of a paper bag. He loved her but, God, she could fuss.

He'd considered staying in London, ignoring the trust. He could simply hand it back to the lawyers to manage for the next fifteen years. But…

"The foundation needs the money, Thea."

"I need you in London, Sutton."

He saw the gleam in her eye, the misery that flashed across her face. And suddenly he realized why she wasn't as enthusiastic about his temporary relocation as he was. He stood up and wrapped his arms around her slim body, then rocked her from side to side. "Are you worried about me interacting with the Ryder-Whites, Thea?"

"No, of course not!"

Yeah, her response didn't sound convincing. He tipped up her chin. "Baby sister, *you* are my family. You and the kids and, at a push, that big lummox you call your husband."

"Also known as your best friend," Thea pointed out.

He waved away her words. "I've never been interested in connecting with my birth family, you know that. Mum and Dad were my parents, and you are my sister. I don't care about the Ryder-Whites."

God, he'd been such a fool as a young man, and if he could go back and yank his head out of his ass, he would. By pulling away and distancing himself from his family, long before his parents' deaths, he'd made his sister feel insecure about his love and his loyalty. Thea sniffed and rested her forehead on his chest.

"Look, Thea, I'm going to get his money whether I want it or not. I don't want it, I don't need it, but the foundation does. And if I need to live in Portland and attend a stupid ball to lay my hands on a hundred and fifty million, then, damn straight that's what I'll do. You know how much the foundation can do with that amount of money."

"We could finally build another children's home, maybe two," Thea told him, sounding excited. "We could also establish more scholarships."

"I need to do this, for the foundation, for Mum and Dad. They'd expect it of me," Sutton told her, resting his chin in her hair.

"Rubbish! They'd be proud of you, but they wouldn't expect it. And you know they would've supported you no matter what you chose to do with the money." She pulled a face and sighed. "They always said it was your right to know your birth parents."

His parents had been shocked when he'd told them he wasn't interested in finding his birth family, surprised at his vehemence on the subject. They'd protested and had spent so much time reassuring him of their support that he'd started to think they wanted to get rid of him. God, he'd been so damn insecure about his parents' love.

And, yeah, his feelings of loss, grief and rejection by his birth parents still lingered. He still occasionally wondered if his parents regretted adopting him, especially since they'd managed to conceive Thea a couple of years after taking him on. Sutton speared his fingers into his hair, wishing he was one of those people who could compartmentalize, who could shove his feelings into mental boxes and lock them away. He tried but didn't always succeed.

He'd made peace with his parents, luckily a few years before they died, and he would've been very happy living out his life not knowing who'd been his birth parents and why they'd given him up for adoption.

He'd had his birth father's identity forced on him, but he had no intention of telling anyone he was Benjamin Ryder-White's son and Callum Ryder-White's nephew. He wasn't interested in becoming the newest member of their wealthy, famous family. The thought made him shudder. He simply wanted Ben's bucks. For the orphans…for all the kids who'd never found their forever home.

But that meant being away from Thea for two months, missing her twin boys' birthday and leaving MarchBent in Sam's capable hands.

"I need to call for a taxi," Thea told him, patting his chest before stepping away.

"No, I'll drive you to the airport," Sutton responded, looking around for the keys to his rental.

He saw them on the desk and pushed them into the back pocket of his jeans.

"I need to make a few calls before we leave, I'll slip into the empty bedroom next door," Thea told him. "Ten minutes?"

"Sure."

Sutton watched her walk away and when she opened the door to leave, she released a little yelp and jumped back. Always protective of his little sister, Sutton bounded across the room and stopped when he saw a slim woman standing in front of Thea, her fist raised as if she was about to knock on the door.

He took in her heart-shaped face, her creamy skin, her made-for-kisses mouth. Her hair—a dark, rich brown—was tucked behind pretty ears and her cheekbones could cut glass. But her eyes... God, her eyes had the ability to drop him to his knees.

They were the color of the Caribbean Sea in bright sunlight. Long, thick black lashes and perfectly sculpted dark eyebrows highlighted the unusual greenish-blue color to perfection.

And talking about perfection... Long legs, a small waist, a very nice set of...

"Hi," Thea chirped. "Sorry to yell, I got a fright!"

The woman smiled, revealing white, even teeth. "No, it's all my fault." Those eyes darted between him and Thea. "I'm sorry, I thought it would be just Mr. Marchant staying with us, but you are, of course, very welcome, Mrs. Marchant. Are you and your husband settling in okay?"

"I'm not staying, but my brother is," Thea said,

stepping back and gesturing to him. "I'm Thea Marchant-Bentley. This is my brother, Sutton Marchant."

The woman's eyes drifted over him with no hint of recognition. "Nice to meet you both. I'm Lowrie Lewis and I run this place."

Low... Ree...it was an unusual name. Sutton folded his arms across his chest and frowned. "I thought Paddy was the manager."

"Paddy owns the business, I run it," Lowrie stated. She glanced around and her eyes widened at the mess in the living area of the suite. "Do you need help getting your study sorted?"

Sutton was about to accept her offer when Thea rolled her eyes and jumped back into the conversation. "Don't touch it or else you'll get growled at! He has a system, or so he says."

"I have a system," Sutton muttered. Sort of. And generally he hated people messing with his stuff, but he wasn't opposed to this sexy woman sticking around a little longer.

"He'll get to it, Lowrie," Thea said, sounding bossy. "He'll ask you to do it, complain and then he'll rearrange everything after you are done, anyway."

God, Thea made him sound like a control freak. And, when it came to his work, he supposed he was.

Lowrie met his eyes and smiled, and Sutton heard his own heartbeat, extra loud in his ears. A long shiver ran up and down his spine and his vision narrowed until she was all that was in it.

Damn. He wanted to haul her into his room, kick

out his sister and find out whether she tasted as good
as she looked.

Ah, *crap*. He didn't need this distraction now.

"What time would you like breakfast in the morning, Mr. Marchant? And when would be a good time
for me to make your bed, tidy up?"

Uh, he couldn't think.

Thea, bless her, jumped into the conversation.
"Call him Sutton, Lowrie. My brother is a writer,
and works and sleeps at weird hours. So maybe you
can play it by ear? Just promise me that if you haven't
seen him in days, then bang on his door and check
that he's still alive, okay?"

Sutton glared at her. "Funny. I only did that once."

"And that was enough for me," Thea retorted. She
pointed a finger at him. "Do not hole up in here for
hours at a time. Take a break, get some fresh air."

He ran ten to fifteen miles a day and tried to
stretch every few hours. He used a dictation program
and when he remembered, did some yoga stretches
an ex-lover once showed him. He wasn't a complete
slug. But Thea liked to fuss and he let her.

"You were going to make calls, Thea," Sutton reminded her.

Thea nodded. "I was. Nice to meet you, Lowrie."

"You, too," Lowrie stated as Thea walked past her.
She glanced at Sutton again and looked at the mess
on his floor, and he saw the infinitesimal shake of
her head.

"It looks bad now but I will get it sorted in a day or
two," Sutton reassured her. And then wondered why.

He was hiring this place at a stupid daily rate and if he wanted to cover every inch in paper, he could. But, for some asinine reason, he didn't want this woman thinking he was a slob.

"Dinner?"

Was she asking him out? As much as he'd love to accept her offer, he had to get Thea to the airport and he'd only be back after eight. "I have to get Thea to the airport, but I'll take a rain check."

She stared at him, her mouth forming a perfect *O*. Then she blushed and rocked on her heels. "Uh, sorry, I meant… I was asking if you were in for dinner tonight? We did say that we would provide dinner and lunch if you gave notice."

Shit. Force of will kept him from reddening, experience kept his expression impassive. "Ah, crossed wires. Sorry. No, I'll grab something. How much notice do you usually need?"

She wrinkled her very pretty nose. "If you are wanting a three-course meal, I'd need to know in the morning. If you require a grilled-cheese sandwich, half an hour."

"Are you a good cook?" he asked, curious.

She shrugged. "I can follow a recipe." Lowrie glanced at her watch. "I need to move along. It was nice meeting you, Mr. Marchant. Let me know if you need anything else."

"Sure," Sutton replied. "And, really, call me Sutton."

She nodded. "Sutton…" She turned to go, then whirled back around to face him. "One more thing…"

He lifted his eyebrows, intrigued by her expression—part pride, part chagrin. "I have a child, he's a year old. He's teething at the moment so if you hear him crying, that's why." She pointed to the ceiling. "I live in the attic space above you, so if you hear me walking or him crying, and we're disturbing you, give me a call and I'll go downstairs or something. My phone number is in the brochure in the desk drawer."

He was a solid sleeper and he rarely heard anything when he was in the zone, so he didn't think it was that big a deal. "Will do."

Lowrie lifted her hand and disappeared in the direction of the stairs. He fought the urge to follow her, reminding himself that he'd made enough of an idiot of himself today. And, yeah, her having a kid made her solidly off-limits. She didn't say whether the kid's father was in the picture, but even if she was a single mom, he didn't date, sleep with or have affairs with women with kids.

Far too much baggage, thank you very much.

Two

Lowrie stepped off the bottom stair onto the harlequin floors of the inn's hallway, grimacing at the drooping heads of the gerbera daisies on the hall table. After removing the almost-dead blooms, she rearranged the greenery and reminded herself to pick up some fresh flowers when she went into town tomorrow.

A massive painting, abstract and colorful, hung on the wall to her right and Lowrie tipped her head to the right, eying the piece. It was fluid, with great composition—she could see the vague outline of a naked woman lying on the settee, but she had to squint to do so.

The colors were just a little off. Cadmium orange deep instead of cadmium orange, ultramarine violet instead of dioxazine purple would've been a better color choice. The slightly different shades would take this picture from good to exceptional.

Turning, Lowrie caught a glimpse of herself in a sleek oval mirror and grimaced at her windblown hair. The combination of being a single mom and busy innkeeper left her looking thin and tired. Lack of sunlight had lightened her pale skin to something resembling a ghost.

She was incredibly surprised that the gorgeous man upstairs had accepted what he thought was a dinner invitation from her earlier. Especially since she looked pale, fragile, wispy…

God, what had happened to that ferociously energetic artist, the one who'd paint all day and night and party all weekend? The girl who'd hop on a plane for Cancún or Cartagena, who'd strip naked and roll around on canvas sheets covered in oil paints? The one who'd lived, breathed and sweated paint and color and art and music and sound?

The one who'd lived at a hundred miles per hour?

Lowrie gripped the edge of the hallway table and stared into the reflection of her eyes, chromium-oxide green edged in viridian. They were her best feature but would be more compelling if they weren't accessorized by blue-black stripes proclaiming she hadn't slept properly in a year.

Lowrie was intensely grateful the rich English guy was the only guest in the place until spring. She needed a slower pace, time to breathe, to play with her baby. She could spend the bulk of the day with Rhan, instead of handing him over to her grandmother at the crack of dawn and running down the street to spend time with him when she could.

A couple of months after Rhan's birth, when she'd returned to Portland, she'd needed work and Paddy, bless him, had pulled her into the inn, given her a place to stay and a job. Her Nonna Jojo and her spinster aunt, Isabel, had scooped up Rhan and lavished him with time, affection and attention, giving Lowrie's battered heart the time and space to heal.

She thanked God every day she was back in Portland, physically better and mentally stronger, and surrounded by the people who loved her...

Lowrie pulled her hair back into a messy knot at the back of her head, securing it with a band she'd slipped onto her wrist hours earlier. She pinched her cheeks to put some color into them and reminded herself to put a tube of lipstick into the drawer of this hall table. Running upstairs to her attic kept her fit and slim but keeping a tube of lipstick down here made sense.

"Is there a reason you are staring at yourself in that mirror?"

Lowrie saw Paddy's hangdog face in the reflection and turned to see her boss, and friend, standing in the doorway to the hall. In his eighties, he had a shock of white hair but his shoulders were rounded and he no longer moved as quickly as he used to. His bright blue eyes were as penetrating as ever.

"Just thinking that I look like a ghost and could do with some lipstick. And maybe blush."

Paddy gave her a long up-and-down look. "You need a haircut and to pick up ten pounds. And, yes, some blush wouldn't hurt."

Wow. "Thanks, I didn't realize I was looking so awful."

"Baby girl, you could dress in a flour sack and you'd still be beautiful, but with a little care you could look stunning." He shrugged, lifting his bony shoulders. "Just calling it like I see it." Paddy tapped his index finger against his cheek. "Would your sudden interest in your appearance have anything to do with the very sexy Englishman upstairs?"

Despite his advanced years, Paddy could still appreciate a sexy man. And, God, Sutton Marchant was Sexy with a capital *S*. Tall, with powerful shoulders and a wide chest, a narrow waist and hips and long, powerful legs. And that face. Up close, it was fantastic and topped with overlong messy hair, burnt umber shot with earthy yellow. His stubble was thicker than she'd thought, his jaw stronger. And his chin more stubborn. But his eyes caught and held her attention. They were manganese blue, a cool, transparent shade with a green undertone. In anger, or high emotion, she thought they'd darken to phthalo blue, one of her favorite colors in the world, elegant and intense.

Lowrie wrinkled her nose. "He is a good-looking guy." She raised her eyebrows. "Gay?"

Paddy, who had come out in the 1970s and never looked back, shook his head. "My gaydar tells me he's a hundred-percent hetero, darling. Why? Are you interested?"

Lowrie snorted. "As if. When Rhan's no-better-than-a-sperm-donor daddy ran out on me in Eureka, I swore I'd avoid the species for the rest of my life."

"That's a bit dramatic, isn't it?"

She shrugged. Maybe. But in her head, every person she ever loved had let her down—her parents, her fiancé, Rex, the aforementioned sperm donor. She'd had her heart broken enough times in a variety of ways, thank you very much.

She didn't think her heart could handle another beating.

"You need to get back on the horse, Lowrie darling."

Lowrie frowned at Paddy. "What does that even mean?"

His intense gaze didn't waver. "You need to date again, sleep with a guy, have some earthshaking sex."

Lowrie fought the urge to slap her hands over her ears. Paddy was the most liberal, open, in-your-face person she knew, but she didn't feel comfortable discussing her sex life—or lack of it—with the octogenarian.

"You need an affair, someone to put some color back into your face."

Despite her parents' open marriage, her wild friends when she was still New York's darling and running with a Bohemian crowd before her pregnancy, she'd never felt comfortable having sex for sex's sake. Hell, she'd only had three lovers in ten years. "Can we not talk about this now, please?"

Paddy shook his head. "When are we going to talk about it?"

"Never?" Lowrie asked, sounding hopeful.

"You are a young, lovely woman who needs to get out of this house, to be in the company of younger people for a change. You need to dress up and feel appreciated. You need to feel like a woman, not a frazzled single mom."

But that was what she was—a frazzled single mom. And she liked spending time with Jojo and Isabel; they were strong, opinionated, wise woman. And Paddy, for all his grumpiness, was fiercely intelligent and widely read. The guests flowing in and out of The Rossi kept her busy.

And Rhan, well, he was her heart.

"Over the next two months, you'll have a great deal more time on your hands as we'll only have one guest to look after."

Lowrie nearly danced on the spot with happiness. "I know! Hiring the inn has cost him a fortune but, God, I'm so grateful for the break."

Paddy narrowed his eyes at her. "And what do you intend on doing with your extra time?"

She shrugged. "Sleep a little later, play with Rhan, paint the empty bedrooms. You said that we could redecorate as well, so I'll be buying new curtains, linens, cushions."

Paddy rolled his eyes. "I was hoping you'd tell me that you'd get a makeover, buy some new clothes, go on a date, fly down to Cancún with some hot man for some fun in the sun."

"That sounds like a plan."

At the sound of the deep voice coming from behind her, Lowrie spun around, her face heating when she saw their only guest standing on the bottom step, unabashedly listening to their conversation. He'd pulled a leather bomber jacket over his hooded sweater and held a pair of gloves in his left hand.

Before either of them could respond, Sutton nodded to Paddy. "Hi, again."

"Are you settled in?" Paddy asked, remembering his innkeeping manners.

"Getting there," Sutton replied, shoving his hands into the pockets of his bomber jacket. "I love this inn with its steep roof, clapboard exterior, the gray shingle roof and black window shutters. Is it old?"

"It was built at the end of the nineteenth century by my ex's ancestors," Paddy replied.

Sutton looked around the double volume hall, his eyes going to the abstract painting Lowrie had been critiquing a few minutes before. "That's a hell of a piece. Is it by a local artist?"

Paddy smiled. "That was one of—"

Lowrie felt hot and cold all over and she spoke over Paddy. "It's by a local artist, but she doesn't paint anymore."

Sutton frowned. "Pity. She's damn good."

There were so many flaws in that painting that sometimes Lowrie couldn't bear to look at it. There were better examples of her art throughout the house, but Paddy and Carlo had declared that piece, called *Woman Floating*, as their favorite.

God, she'd been so young when she painted it. So young. She'd painted the next in the series years later, shortly after she moved into her own studio in Brooklyn. Had she been eighteen? Nineteen? She'd had a futon on the floor, a two-plate stove and a fridge, and the rest of the space was filled with paints and brushes and canvases of every size and description.

That year, before her career had skyrocketed had been, bar none, the happiest of her life. A time when she felt confident and comfortable.

"I hope you don't think I'm abandoning you, Sutton, but I'll be leaving tomorrow for an extended visit to my sister in San Diego."

Sutton nodded. "I'm sure Lowrie and I will be fine without you."

They heard footsteps on the stairs and Sutton turned around to take Thea's heavy leather briefcase. Stepping into the hall, Sutton's sister smiled at Paddy, and surprised Lowrie by putting both hands on her shoulders and kissing her right cheek, then her left.

"Sutton hates guavas and detests gherkins. He's always grumpy in the morning—give him a vat of coffee before you try to talk to him. Take no crap."

"Hey!" Sutton protested, poking her in the side.

"Just calling it like I see it."

"I see you walking to the airport," Sutton grumbled as he strolled to the front door. He opened it and waited for Thea to step into the frigid cold of Maine in late January before following her outside.

When the door closed behind him, Lowrie spun around to look at one of the two men she most admired in the world. Great-Uncle Carlo had been one, Paddy was the other. She loved him, but she didn't much like him at the moment.

"Paddy, what the hell? You didn't tell me you were going away! When did you decide this?"

"Three minutes ago," Paddy calmly replied. "You can handle one guest, can't you?"

Were his eyes twinkling? What was the old man plotting? Lowrie sent him a what-are-you-up-to? glare. "But what about my trip to Cancún?"

"We both know that you no longer have the pep, verve or guts to go to Cancún, darling."

"I still have verve. And pep."

"No, you don't. But I can still be impulsive so that's why I'm going to California. Besides, it's much warmer there."

She tried another tack. "You're leaving me alone in this house with a strange man?"

"He's six-four and muscular—I'm over eighty and frail, so I don't think I'm much protection. And I'm a dedicated pacifist so I have no weapons in the house."

"That's not exactly reassuring!" Lowrie stated, her voice rising.

Paddy placed his hand on her shoulder. "He's a famous author, Lowrie. He writes about serial killers—he isn't one. And I think he's a decent enough guy. He has a straight way of looking you in the eye, saying his piece."

"You met him ten minutes ago."

He shrugged again. "Learned how to size up men in Korea, and it's never failed me yet. You'll be fine.

He's also single and he likes you," he added, his expression mischievous.

Lowrie tossed her hands in the air, completely frustrated. "Are you leaving because you think he will strip me naked and ravage me on the stairs?"

"I live in hope," Paddy told her, patting her shoulder before turning to walk away.

"You are irrational, annoying and interfering!" Lowrie told his departing back. "He's not my type."

Paddy stopped and turned to smile at her. "Of course he is. And that's why you stopped by the mirror and decided you needed lipstick. He's the first man who's made you think of how you look, reminded you that you are a woman. And that's why I'm making myself scarce."

Lowrie stamped the heel of her boot on the hardwood floor. "You don't even like your sister!" she shouted.

"Ah, but I do like her next-door neighbor. I might find myself spending more time at his place than at hers."

Lowrie shoved her hands into her hair, dislodged the knot on the back of her neck and released a string of low curses, most of which she'd learned from Paddy.

"If it has tires and testicles, starter motors and stubble, no matter its age, it's gonna give you trouble," Lowrie muttered, repeating one of Jojo's favorite sayings.

Later that day, Lowrie lit a fire in the fireplace, which was original to the house, and placed the fireguard in front of the flames. Picking up Rhan, she walked over to the bank of long, narrow windows looking out onto the rugged Maine coast. Portland was only ten minutes away, but this house, situated at the end of a long road and at the place where the land ran out, felt isolated.

She wasn't, not really. Jojo's house was a couple of doors down, a scant half mile down the road, but on an evening like this, when snow covered the beach and clouds almost touched the sea, the house felt gloomy and atmospheric.

It almost made her want to pick up a paintbrush, prepare a canvas. Almost but not quite.

Lowrie rocked from side to side, holding Rhan's little fist and dropping kisses on his downy head. He'd been bathed and fed and it was almost time to put him in his bed.

She pulled back to look at him, and saw that his eyelids were heavy, and his face was sleepy-soft. He laid his head on her chest and her heart swelled, growing until she thought it might burst.

She'd heard of a mother's love—had never experienced it from her own mom—but only understood the concept once Rhan had arrived in her life. The love she felt for this little soul was all-encompassing, endless, expansive. He was her life and the reason the sun rose for her every morning, the reason it dropped every night.

He was her everything…

He had Rex's blond hair, her generous mouth, his nose and ears. Rhan's eyes, round and bright blue in his moon-pie face, were all his own. His personality was part bully, part charmer, and she wouldn't have him any other way. He wasn't her clone, or his father's—he was just Rhan, sweet and perfect and wonderful.

And now asleep.

Content to stand in front of the window and watch the snow drift onto the wraparound veranda, Lowrie continued to rock him, the motion as soothing to her as it was to him. Tomorrow Paddy would catch his plane out west and she would be alone with Sutton Marchant. And, really, she wasn't worried about sharing a house with the man. She, like Paddy, knew she was in no danger from him.

And, yes, she had cyberstalked him.

He was thirty-five and after years of working on both Wall Street and the London Stock Exchange, he'd written a beginner's guide to investing that rocketed up the nonfiction bestseller charts. Then he started writing fiction and his star kept climbing.

She was more a historical-romance type of girl—sometimes she even ventured into literary fiction and memoirs—but, thanks to running a busy inn and looking after her child, the minute she opened a book at night, her eyes closed. The last book she'd read cover to cover was *What to Expect When You're Expecting*.

Sutton was, according to the internet, a bestselling author and his gorgeous sister was married to his best friend and partner in his investment firm. He lived in the house he inherited from his parents, situated in the fancy suburb of Knightsbridge, and was a fitness fanatic.

Yeah, that was easy to believe. You didn't get a body like that by being a couch potato.

Why was she so curious about a man she'd only met today, spoken to twice? Maybe it was the hints of sadness she saw in those compelling blue eyes, the suggestion of vulnerability beneath that I'm-a-guy's-guy attitude. He was tough, direct, masculine—but she couldn't help thinking that he was fighting a few hard-to-banish demons.

She knew all about fighting demons.

Lowrie heard the front door opening and closing and cocked her head. Paddy was upstairs in his room, Jojo and Isabel wouldn't wander down here in a snowstorm, so that left Sutton. She expected to hear the sound of boots on the stairs, but her heart rate increased as she heard him crossing the hall.

"Do you mind if I join you?" Sutton asked from the doorway.

She turned, noting the snowflakes in his hair and on his leather-clad shoulders. "Sure, come on in and get warm."

He headed toward the fire, then held out his hands over the fireguard. "Hell of a snowstorm."

Lowrie looked at the gentle falling flakes and smiled. "This? This is nothing. Wait until you experience a blizzard."

"I'll pass, thanks."

Oh, dear. "Sorry, but there's a cold front moving

in next week and they are predicting whiteout conditions."

"Marvelous." Pulling his hands back, he looked at Rhan. "Cute kid."

"I think so." Lowrie nodded her thanks. "He fell asleep about five minutes ago. I need to take him upstairs and put him down. Did your sister get off all right?"

"Yes, thank you."

He shrugged out of his jacket, draped it over the back of a chair and sat down in one corner of the large leather couch. He leaned back his head and closed his eyes. "God, I'd kill for a whiskey," he murmured.

Lowrie headed to the drinks cupboard in the corner and, using one hand, selected a crystal tumbler. Eyeballing a serving, she dashed in a decent amount of Paddy's best whiskey and carried it over to Sutton, then nudged his wrist with the glass.

He opened his eyes—the man had ridiculously long, thick eyelashes—and groaned in appreciation as his fingers wound around the glass. "Thank you." He sipped and sighed. "That's a good whiskey. But if you'd told me where to find it, I could've gotten it myself."

"Not a problem," Lowrie replied. Nice to know that he didn't expect her to wait on him.

Tipping Rhan so that he was on his side, she sat down on the arm of the chair and darted a glance at the fire. It needed another log, but she needed another hand, and if she put Rhan down anywhere other than his crib, he was bound to wake. "Can I ask you to put a couple of logs on the fire?"

"Sure." Sutton stood up and did as she'd asked.

"Thank you. You're welcome to build a fire anytime you choose—there's plenty of wood." Lowrie looked down at her sleeping son. Should she take him upstairs, put him down and return to talk to Sutton about his expectations for the next few months?

Or should she just plow ahead now?

"What's on your mind, Lowrie?"

Right, that answers that question. "I thought maybe we should have a chat about what you expect? You have paid us an extraordinary amount of money to have the exclusive use of this place, so I just want to make sure you are comfortable."

He looked around, taking in the big, squishy furniture, the fresh flowers and the incredible art—some of it hers—on the wall. "It's a pretty comfortable place. It feels like a home."

It was. It had been Carlo and Paddy's home long before it had been turned into an inn, and her great-grandparents' house before that.

"Obviously, I'll make your bed every day and do your laundry, make you breakfast. That's standard. But what about lunch and dinner, snacks?" She glanced at the whiskey bottle. "What do you like to drink, eat? Are you allergic to anything? You saw the small study attached to your room but would you prefer to work somewhere else? There are another six bedrooms you can work from, or, if you prefer, you can take over the small library. I use a desk in there but if you want privacy, I can relocate."

Sutton picked up his glass and took a sip of whiskey. "Where's the library?" He frowned. "Can I get you a glass of wine? Something else to drink?"

She appreciated the offer but shook her head. "I'm good, thank you." She nodded to a door behind him. "The library is through there."

Sutton, carrying his glass, walked across the room and stepped into her favorite space in the house. It was an L-shaped room covered in bookcases and had, in her opinion, the best views of the peninsula, beach and forest. She'd be sad to lose her working spot—the window seat was also her favorite place to take a break—but Sutton had paid for the privilege of working wherever he wanted to.

"This is a stunning room."

She heard the sincerity in his voice and his appreciation made her smile. He popped his head around the doorframe. "This is an unbelievable collection of books as well."

"My great-uncle Carlo was an avid reader," Lowrie explained. She stood up, walked around the chair and sat down properly, allowing Rhan to settle in her lap, against her chest. Her arms moaned in gratitude. Her boy was getting heavy.

"Could we move another desk in here?" Sutton called out.

Lowrie dampened her disappointment at losing her favorite room. "I'm sure we can," she replied. When he walked back into the room, she pulled up a smile. "After all, you need another desk for all your books and stuff."

"Ah, no. I was just wanting a desk for my laptop, for when I want to write in there. And I think I'll want to write in there quite often."

She didn't understand. "But then why do you need another desk?"

He sat down again and placed his ankle on his opposite knee. "You use that desk and I can't kick you out. If you don't mind sharing, I'll help you move another desk in there for me to use. There's more than enough room and your presence won't bother me." He sent her a slow, lazy smile that had her stomach doing slow rolls. "I can write on trains, planes, and in busy, noisy coffee shops. Once I'm in the zone, it takes a bomb to disrupt me."

She couldn't help her grin. "So you're not a precocious writer then?"

"Have you met my sister? Do you think she'd allow me to be?"

True. Thea didn't look like she took any nonsense from anyone. "If you'll help me move the desk, I'm happy to share the space. But I will go outside the room for calls."

Sutton nodded his thanks. He stared at his whiskey glass and then at the fire, his thoughts a long way off. She didn't want to disturb him, but...

"I do still need answers about lunch and dinner, what you like to drink and snack on, what coffee you like and I need to give you a key to the house."

"Paddy already did that, when I arrived," Sutton

told her. "Thea wasn't joking when she said that I work crazy hours so I can't give you a definite answer about lunch and dinner. Sometimes I work through, forgetting about food. Sometimes I want something to eat at three in the morning. What time do you and Paddy eat?"

"When guests ask for dinner, we eat at seven," Lowrie told him. "But Paddy is going to visit his sister so it'll just be you and me." She looked away from him, inexplicably embarrassed. "I hope you're okay with that?"

He took a while to answer her and eventually Lowrie looked at him. As soon as their eyes met, he spoke again. "I think the question should be whether you are comfortable in the house with *me*?"

"But you're the guest."

"But you're a woman, half my size," Sutton said, sitting up straight. He leaned forward and held her eyes. "I would never hurt you, Lowrie, but I don't expect you to take my word on that."

Yet, strangely, she did. She pulled in a deep breath and nodded. "I'm fine with you staying, Sutton."

"Good," he replied, his tone matter-of-fact. "I'm not allergic to anything and I eat everything, bar the aforementioned guavas and gherkins. If you make yourself something for supper, make extra and if I don't respond when you call, leave it out for me to find. If you can buy some frozen meals for the times you don't feel like cooking, that would be great. I'll have an order of whiskey and wine delivered, I like both. I run most days, sometimes at night, sometimes during the day." He glanced toward the windows and pulled a face at the falling snow. "Is there a gym anywhere close by?"

"Portland is ten minutes away, but if you only need the basics, there's a minigym next to the pool house."

"You have a pool? Where?" Sutton demanded.

"Jeez, didn't Paddy show you around when you arrived?"

Sutton stood up to pour himself another drink. "I told him I'd see everything later and time ran away from me."

"I'll take you on a tour in the morning. Yes, there's a lap pool, to the side of the house. It's heated so you can swim anytime you want." She swam most mornings, but the pool was big enough for the two of them. "The gym is next to the pool and we have a treadmill, a weight bench, a couple of other machines. It'll do if you aren't superfussy."

"Not fussy," Sutton assured her. So far, he was turning out to be the dream guest. She was sure, as they got to know each other, that would change. Nobody was as easy and amiable as Sutton Marchant appeared to be. And living with someone stripped away the masks people wore.

"I didn't choose this inn, but damn, this spot isn't too shabby," Sutton said, sliding down in his seat and stretching out those long, long legs.

What did he mean by that? Lowrie pulled her eyes off his muscular thighs and flat stomach to ask, but Rhan let out a little cry and wiggled in her arms. She glanced down and saw his eyes fluttering. Rhan only liked to be cuddled for a set amount of time and then he wanted to be in his crib, where he could stretch out.

"I need to put him down," Lowrie said, scooting to the edge of her seat. She started to push herself up and was surprised when Sutton stood up and held out his hand for her to grip. Placing her hand in his, he pulled her and her son up with ease.

"Thank you," she murmured. She looked up, into his eyes, which were intensely blue and glittering with an emotion she couldn't identify. Whatever it was, it made her feel warm and tingly and a little strange.

Lovely strange. Attracted strange.

Which wasn't good.

Lowrie tightened her grip on Rhan and forced a polite smile onto her face. "If you haven't eaten, I have beef soup on the stove. There's also sourdough bread."

"Thanks, but I'm fine. I grabbed a pizza at the airport," Sutton replied.

Lowrie nodded, murmured an "excuse me" and walked past him, cursing herself for feeling disappointed. He might be her only guest but he was still a guest and distance should be maintained.

No, physical and emotional distance *had* to be maintained.

Whenever she got close to people her heart ended up being bruised and battered and she'd never let that happen again.

Three

Penelope

Penelope dug her nails into her biceps and looked at her husband of thirty-plus years, the icy fingers of fear skittering up and down her spine. How did one reveal a three-decades-old secret? How could she be as open with him as he'd been with her?

He'd just informed her that he wanted to acknowledge his son, a son he'd had with his father's personal assistant before Penelope and James were married.

Because she was human, she wanted to rail at James for keeping his son a secret, for never telling her that he'd had an affair with Emma. But she couldn't, not when her own secrets eclipsed his…

It's not a competition, Penelope.

James thought she was scared of the consequences of him acknowledging Garrett Kaye as his son. James's father, Callum, would push James out of the business and them out of the family. But she agreed with her husband's plan. Like him, she was tired of being dictated to by Callum Ryder-White.

"Walking away from Callum doesn't scare me, James," she said, a shrill laugh following her words.

"Then what does, Pen?"

"Your reaction to what I'm about to tell you. Sit down, darling, you're not the only one who has a bombshell to drop."

James perched on the edge of his chair, his eyes wary. Her eyes were a more unusual shade of light blue, surrounded by a darker ring. She'd been complimented on them all her life, but neither of her girls had inherited her intense eye color. No, the only person who had the same eyes was that little boy so long ago...

"Talk to me, Pen. There's nothing we can't do together." James looked and sounded earnest.

Oh, God, he was so sweet and, despite closing in on sixty, was still too kindhearted. There were some things that couldn't be solved with a smile and a hug, things that could come back to haunt them.

The son she gave up for adoption was a case in point.

Despite so many decades passing, she still expected him to drop back into her life, and if he did, she knew the lives of all the people she loved would never be the same again.

Penelope looked out the window and her eyes immediately went to the patch of trees by the tennis court, overlooking the cove. The memory of that long-ago day was still crystal clear.

After a week-long affair, she hadn't been able to make contact with the man who'd impregnated her and then, not unexpectedly, she'd seen him again at the Ryder-White Fourth of July celebration eighteen months later. He'd made a stupid comment about her engagement, something about keeping it in the family, and she responded by railing at him for ignoring her many calls and letters.

He'd curled his lip, told her she'd been a way to pass the time, to alleviate his boredom. And that, by sleeping with her, he'd finally came to terms with the fact that he preferred men.

Hurt and anger had crashed over her like a tidal wave. Being young and vain, she thought he was just trying to hurt her, and needing to wound him in return, she'd told him—a little gleefully—that she'd given up his son for adoption.

His immediate and visceral anger had scared her. How dare she make that decision without him? he'd snarled. He'd wanted to know where the boy was, what was his name. Caught off guard by his intense reaction, she'd told him about the agency in London and the name of her case worker. Then, two months later—after coming out to his family and creating a storm of epic proportions—he was dead.

Although he'd never disclosed that he had a child, Penelope had no doubt that in those two months he'd made plans. He wasn't the type to leave events to play themselves out.

She'd made sure to leave her contact details with the agency, was fairly certain that her son's father would've done the same. So why hadn't her boy contacted her or contacted his father's family? It made no sense.

"Pen?"

She didn't know if she could bear to see the disappointment on James's face. He might not have been her first choice for a husband, but she'd come to love him. She liked his kindness, his patience and his affectionate personality. She found his new quest for independence from his controlling father sexy. She didn't want to lose her husband, and she feared that revealing her secret might lead to exactly that.

She wasn't ready, wasn't strong enough, couldn't be on her own...

Penelope lifted her fingers to her forehead, conscious of her pounding head and her dry mouth. She lifted her eyes to meet James's, feeling awful about the confusion on his face. He was waiting, but she wasn't ready, not yet.

She waved her hand in the air. "I do have something to tell you, but... I can't, not yet."

James placed his hands on his knees, disappointment running across his face. "Can you tell me why not? Don't you trust me?"

"I *do* trust you, I just need some time. Everything is moving so fast and things are changing."

"You've never been good at change, Pen."

Oh, God, wasn't that the truth? "I know. I thought I was ready to tell you, but I'm not."

James nodded, staring at his hands. He pulled in a deep breath, the way he always did when he had unpleasant news to break, something tough to say. "Pen, in case you are thinking of confessing to past… indiscretions, I'm begging you not to. I don't need to know, any more than you need to know about mine." He dragged his hand down his face. "I think we might be getting to a point of finally having an honest relationship. Let's not spoil this new beginning, okay?"

She swallowed her hysterical laugh. Affairs? That's where he thought she was going? If only. But because he'd given her an out, she'd take it. So she nodded, tried to smile. "I have a headache. I think I might go and lie down for a while, wrap my head around the idea that I have a ridiculously wealthy, successful stepson."

James stood up and placed his lips on her forehead. He kept them there for a long time before stepping back. "There's nothing we can't handle, Pen. Just remember that, okay?"

Oh, God, he really believed that. But some things, as Pen knew, weren't so easily dealt with. Or forgiven.

A week later, Lowric was surprised to hear boots heading toward the kitchen, where she was making herself and the very elusive Sutton Marchant a chicken salad, in between feeding Rhan pureed vegetables.

She looked up as Sutton stepped into the massive

country kitchen, dressed in a pair of designer jeans and a black sweater, sleeves pushed up past his elbows. A pair of wire-framed glasses on his nose made him look like a very sexy professor.

"Hey," she said.

Sutton surprised her by laying a gentle hand on Rhan's head as he passed to sit down at the big table in the center of the kitchen. "Hi back."

Lowrie pointed her knife to the salad she was making. She was becoming used to making food, covering it with Saran Wrap and leaving it in the fridge, only to find the empty plate in the dishwasher a couple of hours later. "Would you like some lunch?" she asked him, expecting him to say no.

"Yeah, that would be great," Sutton replied. "Thanks."

Wow, they were going to share their first meal after a week of living together. No, not living together, sharing the same house. She was his temporary housekeeper, nothing more, nothing less.

Lowrie fed Rhan a spoon of baby goop then carried on assembling the salad. "How's the writing going?"

Sutton pulled a face. "Better. I've just finished edits on a book due next week."

Sutton got up, reached for a glass and shoved it under the tap. After drinking, he filled it again and asked Lowrie if he could pour her something.

She refused, fed her little openmouthed bird and started to shred cold chicken.

Sutton leaned against the counter opposite her and

crossed his ankles. "What do you know about the Ryder-Whites?"

Lowrie looked at him, frowning. "Portland's princesses?"

"Who?"

"That's what they call Kinga and Tinsley, the Ryder-White daughters... Portland's princesses."

"They are that well-known?" Sutton asked, resting his glass against his huge biceps. She'd love to see him shirtless... Hell, naked. She wanted to see if his stomach was as ridged as she imagined, whether his erection was as impressive—

Dear God, it's one thirty on a Tuesday afternoon, Lewis!

Maybe Paddy was right—maybe she did need to have an affair, to get back into the groove. But the only man she could imagine getting naked with was her guest. Which wasn't going to happen.

She met his eyes and saw that he was waiting for an answer. Right, they'd been talking about the Ryder-Whites.

"The Ryder-Whites are East Coast nobility," Lowrie explained. "They have the bluest of blue blood and can trace their family tree right back to the first European settlers in Yarmouth. Why are you asking about them?"

"Ah, because I am attending their Valentine's Day Ball this Saturday?"

Her knife stopped abruptly and she looked up at him, her mouth agape. "Seriously?"

He shrugged. "Yeah."

Right, she didn't know much about the ball, but she did know it was one of the world's most exclusive social events. Princes and celebs, billionaires and sheikhs, fought for tickets. The price of the tickets were a closely guarded secret and it was said that if you had to ask how much they cost, you couldn't afford to attend.

"I've been meaning to look them up, but I've been swamped. What do the daughters do?" Sutton asked.

Lowrie had only been back in Portland for a year and she'd been far too busy to keep up with local gossip. But, invariably, there were some things you couldn't help hearing, especially since her grandmother and aunt were huge followers of the local news. "They run the PR division of Ryder International. They are responsible for organizing and hosting the Valentine's Day Ball in Manhattan."

Sutton's attention sharpened. "It's in Manhattan?" he demanded.

"For someone who's forked out a lot of cash to attend the social event of the year, you don't know much about it," Lowrie commented, more than a little confused.

"You are not wrong," Sutton conceded. "In my defense, I've been snowed under and left the arrangements to Thea."

Rhan banged his little hand on the table and Lowrie hastily shoved another spoon of food into his mouth. He grinned at her and gummed his food.

"Do not get in the way of my son and his food," Lowrie said, then returned to the subject at hand.

"The first Ryder-White ball was hosted decades ago by Callum Ryder-White's brother, I can't remember his name, and it's morphed into an annual, not to be missed, event. To be fair, the ball might be horribly exclusive but it does raise lots of money for their foundation."

"They have a foundation?"

"They are the richest family on the East Coast, Sutton—of course, they have a foundation. I think the brother set that up, too," Lowrie said, reaching for ingredients to make a simple salad dressing. That done, she pulled two bold blue plates out from the cabinet and set the table. Sutton sent her a smile of thanks as he pulled his phone from the back pocket of his jeans. "Give me a minute," he asked.

Lowrie shrugged, scooped up the rest of Rhan's food and popped the spoon in his mouth. He grabbed the spoon out of her hand and proceeded to bite down on it. Damn, he always did that when his teeth were bothering him. She hoped they weren't in for another night short on sleep.

"Thea, hi," Sutton said. He listened for a moment, smiled and leaned back.

They spoke for a few minutes and then Sutton raised the subject of the ball. "I remember seeing an email but confirm that all the arrangements are in place for me to attend Ryder International's Valentine's Day Ball?"

Despite being across the table, Lowrie heard Thea's reply. "They are. It wasn't easy getting a ticket at the last minute but I pulled some strings, dropped a couple of names, used your title."

"You have a title?" Lowrie demanded.

Sutton's reply was to create a tiny space between his thumb and index finger. Was he an earl? A marquess, a viscount? Her familiarity with aristocratic English titles was due to all those historical romances she'd once had the time to read.

Lowrie dished up some salad, tossed some dressing over it and dug in. Sutton shrugged, told Thea that she was on speakerphone with Lowrie in the room and placed his phone on the table next to his glass.

"How much was the ticket?" Sutton asked, winking at Lowrie. She leaned forward, curious to know the answer, and lifted both her hands to indicate ten thousand dollars. He shook his head and mouthed, *Fifty.*

"Before I tell you, I want to remind you that you said I had to pay what I had to, that it was imperative that you go…" Thea said, sounding a little choked up.

"Yeah, yeah…how much, Thea?"

"Because you bought it so late, the week of the event, you had to pay a penalty," Thea explained. "The ticket cost two hundred and fifty thousand dollars."

Sutton coughed, choked and reached for his water. "What?" he croaked, his eyes wide. Lowrie's mouth dropped open as well.

"That's the cost of a ticket, Sutton," Thea replied. "As I keep saying, it's a premier social event."

"It's bloody highway robbery," Sutton sputtered.

"If it helps, all the money from the ticket sales go to their foundation. They get sponsorships and Ryder International pays a hefty price for hosting the ball," Lowrie told him, trying to wrap her head around the fact that Sutton could afford to spend a quarter million on one evening's entertainment. "I heard that from my grandmother. She follows local news, and the Ryder-Whites in particular."

"Why?" Sutton asked her, after disconnecting his call to Thea.

Lowrie handed Rhan his teething ring. "Why what?"

"Why does she follow the Ryder-Whites in particular?"

Lowrie laid down her fork, sat back and looked at him. "I have no idea, actually. My great-uncle Carlo, Jojo's brother, was the same. They were, to put it mildly, obsessed with everything that family did."

"Did they know Benjamin Ryder-White?" Sutton asked, in a tone that was so casual it immediately raised Lowrie's curiosity.

"Is that the name of Callum Ryder-White's brother?" Lowrie asked. Seeing Sutton's nod, she shrugged. "I don't think they knew him."

They ate in a silence, although it was occasionally broken by Rhan banging the spoon on the plastic tray of his baby chair.

"Two hundred and fifty K," Sutton said mournfully after he'd demolished most of his salad. "I could've bought a holiday home for that, or a nineteen-sixties Shelby Cobra."

The most expensive painting Lowrie sold, at the height of her so-called fame, was for a hundred thousand, but after Kyle, her agent-slash-fiancé, and her gallery-owner mother took their cut, she only saw just over half of that.

Lowrie's eyes widened. She assumed he was wealthy but not crazy rich. "Sorry, but that's stupid money."

She could buy an art shop with that money. Or a gallery. An amazing painting or sculpture by an incredible artist...

"It is," Sutton agreed.

"Then why are you going?" Lowrie demanded.

"Reasons," Sutton replied, before finishing his salad. He pulled a funny face at Rhan, who laughed, and returned his attention to his food. Right, he didn't want to explain his interest in the Ryder-Whites. Message received. Loud and clear.

Sutton caught the shadowy figure out of the corner of his eye and slowed down, lifting his head out of the water to watch Lowrie slip into the pool beside him. He saw that she was wearing a one-piece swimsuit, and a cap over her long hair, hoping to keep it relatively dry. But it was her body that caught his attention—tall and slim, with muscled legs and arms, and a flat stomach. And, yeah, great breasts.

Sutton ducked his head back into the warm water and powered to the other end of the pool, easily passing Lowrie. She had good form, he noticed—much better than his. It was easy to see that she'd had some training.

Being a night owl, he frequently worked and exercised late at night, but he could afford to play with his working hours. As an innkeeper, Lowrie couldn't, and because it was past midnight, he wondered why she wasn't in bed asleep. Pulling into a breaststroke, he noticed the baby monitor on her towel quite close to the pool. He slowed down, drew level with her and spoke. "Do you often take midnight swims?"

She grimaced. "Rhan is teething and he woke up crying. I gave him some pediatric pain medicine and he's asleep but I'm now awake. You?"

"Things."

He caught her smile. "Writing things or Ryder-White things?" she asked.

God, she was perceptive! He thought about lying, then did a mental shrug. "Both."

"Why are you so interested in the Ryder-Whites?" Lowrie asked him, her breath visible in the cold air. "Are you using them for research?"

It was as good as an excuse as any but he didn't give her a definite answer. "Are they that interesting?"

"Some would think so," Lowrie quietly replied. "I'm just not impressed with fame and fortune."

He believed that. She knew he was a writer and he had no doubt that she'd done a little research on him. Even the most cursory of internet searches would tell her that he was one of the most successful authors around. Hiring out the inn and instructing Thea to pay for his ticket to the ball would tell her that he was seriously wealthy.

Yet, she'd never once suggested she was impressed. That both annoyed him and intrigued him.

He was used to woman falling over themselves to date him, to pull him into some sort of relationship or arrangement. Uninterested in settling down, he'd had a lot of practice dodging them. But Lowrie treated him as just another bloke, someone who could pay a king's ransom to have an empty house and give her a minibreak from cooking and cleaning.

Sutton did a tumble turn at the wall and sped up into a fast freestyle, leaving Lowrie behind. But his thoughts remained on her. She hadn't always been in the hospitality game, of that he was sure. He wondered where she'd gone to college and what she'd studied, where she'd worked before she landed at The Rossi. He could see her as a kindergarten teacher. She was incredibly patient with her son. Or he could see her working as an event planner, as nothing seemed to ruffle her composure.

She was definitely more of a people person than he was, but he'd noticed that sometimes, especially when she was looking out at the incredible view of the storm-tossed ocean, she had a look in her eye that suggested she was miles away, in the zone. Creatives, he smiled, easily recognized members of their own tribe.

Sutton increased his pace, irritated that she was taking up so much of his mental headspace. He was here to fulfill the conditions of the will so he could donate his birth father's money to his parents' charities. He just needed to hang out at the inn for another seven weeks and attend the Valentine's Day ball, and then he would be done with the situation.

And make his parents proud.

That hadn't been his goal in his late teens and twenties, he'd be the first to admit that. In hindsight, he knew that his parents had treated him and Thea equally, and even back then, he'd intellectually understood that to be true. But deep inside, way down, a small voice insisted that they had to love her more because Thea was *theirs*. They made her and she carried their blood.

When Thea did something amazing—aced a test or nailed a dance routine—he stepped back, watching to see if they praised her more, rewarded her in some way that they didn't him. He couldn't remember a single instance of inequality, but the thought that he was a cuckoo in the nest refused to go away.

Instead, that feeling had grown bigger and bigger and he started to put more distance between himself and his parents. By the time he left school, he was barely on speaking terms with his mum and dad. In his twenties, he pushed away his guilt at his lack of contact and concentrated on establishing a kick-ass career in finance.

He'd dodged their calls, missed birthday celebrations and holidays, always finding something better to do, somewhere else to be. He worked sixty-to-eighty-hour weeks, often worked weekends too, and used his schedule as an excuse to avoid his parents and sister.

Yeah, he felt guilty but, wrapped up in himself, he figured they were better off without him.

He found solace in writing and when Sam, his oldest friend, became frustrated by dealing with clients who didn't know the difference between a unit trust and a share, he suggested Sutton write a book for beginner investors. He did, had it published and it was a runaway success. He acquired an agent, banged out three chapters of a thriller, had that picked up and a year later he was working as a full-time writer.

It took nearly ten years and his father rocking up on his doorstep and giving him a come-to-Jesus talk that yanked him back into the family fold and opened the door to a new relationship with his parents. Not being a talker, he never explained his insecurities about being adopted, but their relationship did improve dramatically. He had lunch with his mum, played golf with his dad, made every family occasion for two years. He thought he'd have another thirty, forty years with them but, on a sunny afternoon in June, they died when a truck slammed into their side of the car he'd been driving.

They'd been killed instantly and he walked away with minor scratches.

He'd wasted so much time second-guessing their love, second-guessing them. But, despite his confusion, he'd never once in the ten years they'd been estranged, or before or after, wanted to find his birth parents. He had a family; he just hadn't known how to relate to them. And a scant two years after he realized that all they'd wanted from him was his time and attention, they were taken from him.

And his world fell apart.

Completely and indescribably.

It had taken him a long time to crawl out from under the grief, to get back to work, to start living again. He and Thea grew closer, and he was grateful that she never once blamed him for the accident. But it left him with a series of invisible scars and a couple of hard truths.

He'd had a family and had lost it. Thea, Sam and the twins were his family now and they were all he needed. He never wanted to lose someone he loved again. And, this was harder to admit—although he knew his parents loved him, he still didn't know *how* much they loved him. Less than Thea? The same? Did they regret adopting him, especially once they knew they could conceive naturally? Would they have liked a biological son?

He never wanted to question someone's love for him again, so it was easier not to love, to keep his circle small, to stay away from the what-ifs and the doubts and the am-I-good-enoughs.

Sutton felt Lowrie tug on his ankle and he abruptly stopped, dropped his feet so that they hit the floor of the pool and looked across to her. "What?"

"You've been swimming for almost an hour, Sutton, and at a hell of a pace. Enough now."

He looked at his waterproof watch, saw that she was right and noticed that his chest was heaving, that his arms felt heavy and his legs tired. He'd been pushing himself harder than he thought, and he'd been so wrapped up in his thoughts that he'd lost track of time and what he was doing to his body. While he hated being told what to do, he admitted she was right. It was time to stop.

He swam over to her and watched her as she climbed out of the pool, reaching for the warm toweling robe that was lying on a nearby chair. The air temperature hovered around freezing, so he was happy to stay in the warm water and watch her pull her robe over her lovely body, then shove her feet into slippers. She pulled off her cap, allowing her damp hair to fall to her shoulders.

"Damn, it's cold," she muttered, scooping up her baby monitor. She rocked from foot to foot, peering down at him in the low light. "I'm going to make myself a boozy hot chocolate. Do you want one?"

Hell, yes.

"I'll see you in the kitchen in ten minutes."

Sutton glanced at his watch again and saw that it was close to one in the morning. It was, he decided, the perfect time for booze and chocolate.

Four

Sutton offered to build a fire while she made the hot chocolate and Lowrie agreed. She ran upstairs, thought about changing into jeans and a nice sweater. Nope, Sutton would think she was trying too hard, that she was trying to impress him, so she pulled on her favorite pair of men's pajamas and fluffy socks. She towel-dried her hair and left it to fall as it would, into a tumble of curls.

She peered into the mirror of her bathroom and decided that she definitely needed a facial, to shape her eyebrows and trim her hair. There was nothing like having a sexy man in the house to realize that you looked like a wreck.

Not that she was sure he even saw her as a woman. Oh, there were times when she felt his eyes on hers but he kept his expression so impassive she had no idea what he was thinking. She had stretch marks on her tummy and her boobs definitely weren't as perky as they had been five years ago.

Why are you even thinking like this, Lewis?

She wasn't looking for a man or a relationship and even if she was, Sutton had No Entry signs flashing in his eyes. If, somehow, she did get naked with him, it would be on a just-for-fun basis.

Could she do that? Could she be that live-for-the-moment girl? She didn't know. She wasn't sure she wanted to find out.

What she didn't want to do was fall for another unsuitable man. Her fiancé had been unaffectionate, controlling and too ambitious, happy to use her hard work and talent to enrich his own pockets. When she told him that she was taking a break from art, that she wasn't going to exhibit for the next few years, he'd dropped her like a hot coal, taking her cash with him when he walked.

Her parents, on hearing the same news, also lost their shit.

Lowrie tossed ingredients into the pot, threw in a decent amount of liquor and stirred. She was tired but also wired, and she hoped the hot chocolate would help her sleep. And that Rhan wouldn't wake up at the ass crack of dawn. She needed a solid six, maybe eight, hours of sleep to feel human again.

Lowrie poured the hot chocolate into mugs and took them into the sitting room. Sutton, dressed in a pair of navy track pants and a long sleeved T-shirt, was crouched in front of the fire, poking the logs with a poker.

Despite the thick windows, she could hear the sound of the waves pounding the rocks, and heard the house settle and sigh. God, she loved it here.

And drinking hot chocolate late at night with a hot guy wasn't a bad way to pass the time, either.

Lowrie handed Sutton his cup and curled into the corner of the couch, tucking her feet under her butt. She wrapped her hand around her cup as he settled his big frame next to her, his bare feet pointed toward the fire. He lifted his cup to his mouth and Lowrie waited, interested to see his reaction.

His eyebrows lifted momentarily, but, to his credit, he took another sip.

When he looked at her, she saw glinting amusement in his eyes. "When you said boozy hot chocolate I expected whiskey or rum, not chili and…tequila?"

She laughed. "I got the recipe from a bartender I follow on social media. Do you like it?"

He looked at his cup, considering her question. "I do, actually," he told her. "It's different. So, do you always take midnight swims?"

"Not that often and rarely in winter. I thought a long swim would make me tired. I'm surprised you aren't swaying on your feet, since you swam for close to an hour and at top speed."

"I always do when I've got a lot on my mind."

"Your new book?"

"That's part of it," Sutton replied, an answer that told her nothing.

He wasn't a guy who easily let people in, and Lowrie knew he wasn't going to spill his soul, but a part of her wished he would. He needed a friend, a nonjudgmental someone who'd give him another perspective, a differing opinion. But he didn't seem the type who told his secrets to strangers…or anyone.

"Did you ever consider giving your son up for adoption?"

His question was so out of the blue that she jerked in surprise, spilling a couple of drops of hot chocolate onto her hand. She grimaced and placed her cup on the side table to her left. She started to stand up to go wash her hand, when Sutton lifted his T-shirt, giving her a glimpse of his rock-hard abs, and gently smoothed the fabric across her hand. "Okay?"

"Sure, but you've now dirtied your shirt."

"It's a few drops, not a deluge," Sutton told her, wiping her hand again. He was so warm, and his scent—a mixture of a citrus cologne and chlorine from the pool—drifted up her nose. Sitting back, he stretched out his legs, crossing his feet at the ankles.

"I'm sorry if my question startled you. I'm being nosy—you don't have to answer me."

"No, I don't mind. It was just unexpected. Ah, did I ever want to give him up for adoption? Well, in those first few weeks after hearing I was pregnant, I considered all the options. My boyfriend at the time, well, he wanted me to get an abortion and he pushed pretty hard for that to happen. I refused. I'm pro-choice, but my choice was to keep my baby."

Sutton stared at the fire, but Lowrie knew he was listening. "I did think about adoption, for a few weeks. But once I felt him kick, I fell in love with him and I didn't want anyone else raising him but me. He was mine, you know?"

Sutton turned to look at her, his expression enigmatic. "How long did your guy stick around for?"

"Until I went into labor," Lowrie answered, her voice cracking just a little. "He called an ambulance for me, told me that he'd follow as soon as he locked up the house." It still hurt. It shouldn't but it did. "I waited, and waited some more. I called him and his phone went straight to voice mail. An hour passed, then two, then three. Eight hours after leaving the apartment, Rhan was born, but my boyfriend didn't show. When I went back home, he'd cleared out his stuff and disappeared."

Sutton released a low series of curse words, and because he was a writer, his insults were intensely creative.

"I think that when I went into labor, it got very real. Rex was a Peter Pan character and he couldn't cope with the idea of being a father, being responsible."

"Does he, at the very least, pay child support?" Sutton demanded.

"Ah, well, I'd ask him, but I'd need to find him first." And didn't she sound like a fool admitting that? "I tried to track him down, but he ditched his phone, scrubbed his social-media accounts and simply dropped out of my life. Judging by the fact that I cannot find a Rex Hensley anywhere in California—he said he was born in Orange County—I can only assume he gave me a false name."

Sutton stared at her, his expression bemused. "This sounds like something that would happen in a book."

"All too real, I'm afraid. So, Rhan is mine, and I'm good with that."

"How did you get from California to here?"

Lowrie took a sip of her drink, enjoying the kick of chili against the taste of tequila and warm, rich chocolate. "I called Jojo, my grandmother. She and her oldest daughter, Isabel, who is my mom's sister, flew out the day Rhan was born. They packed up my meager possessions while I held Rhan and sobbed."

"Did you love him?"

Now that was a hell of question.

"God, what is love? What does the concept even mean? He was fun, sociable, charismatic and compelling."

"And if he walked back into your life tomorrow?" Sutton asked.

"I'd kick him in the balls and show him the door."

Sutton's lips twitched, as if he was trying to hold back a smile. When he turned to face her again, his expression was remote and altogether too serious. "I'm glad Rhan stayed with you, that you didn't give him up for adoption."

She wrinkled her nose. "Me, too. It's been tough but Jojo and Isabel are my safety net. They've given me so much support. Paddy gave me a job, a place to stay and something to do."

He played with her fingers and Lowrie looked down at her hand, expecting to see tiny fireworks exploding on her skin. "I was adopted, and while I loved my parents, I didn't like being adopted."

Uh…what? Wow, he was opening up.

"I—"

"Why didn't you call your mother when you went into labor? Why your grandmother?" Sutton asked, dropping her hand and reaching for his hot chocolate.

And he'd slammed that door closed again. Well, what did she expect? For him to reveal his deepest secrets? She knew that wasn't going to happen.

"Uh…well, my mother and I are at odds. And because I'm at odds with her, I'm also at odds with my father."

"Been there, done that," Sutton murmured. "What did you do?"

She leaned forward and punched his biceps. It had as much effect as a bee banging against a glass window. "Why do you think I was the one who did something?"

"Because I messed up in my twenties—it's what your twenties are for."

She mock glared at him. "For your information, I wasn't at fault."

"Tell me what happened," Sutton gently commanded.

"You're awfully curious about my life," Lowrie grumbled.

He smiled, unrepentant. "I'm a writer, I'm curious about everything."

"If I tell you, will you put it in a book?"

"It depends how interesting your story is," he replied. "Most people think their lives are interesting but they rarely are. Does your story involve skeletons in cupboards or dead bodies?"

"Literally or figuratively?"

He laughed, a sound as rich, deep and dark as her chili-tequila hot chocolate. Amused, he looked a lot younger, his eyes crinkling at the corner and his lips revealing straight, white teeth. He had a great smile, Lowrie thought.

She wanted to know how it felt under her lips. Lowrie felt her nerves tingling, and that secret place between her legs throbbed. The urge to erase all distance between them pummeled her. She needed to touch and explore.

There were a million reasons why kissing him would be a bad move but she didn't care. For the next few minutes she wanted to feel alive, to feel like a woman, sexy and confident.

"I'm sorry, I have to," she told him, pushing up so that she was kneeling on the couch.

"Have to what?" Sutton asked as she swung her thigh over his and settled into his lap. She lifted both her hands to hold his cheeks, loving the feel of his stubble on her palms.

"Kiss you." Lowrie pulled back to look at him. "Is that okay?"

His big hands gripped her hips, his fingertips burning into her skin through the fabric of her pajamas.

This was a mistake. She knew it was. She wasn't mentally ready to dive into an anything with anybody, but his mouth was a temptation she couldn't resist. Just one kiss, so she could stop wondering, stop fantasizing...

Lying to yourself, Lewis. You know you want more than a kiss.

But a kiss was all she could have.

"This works better if you actually kiss me instead of just staring at my mouth," Sutton murmured, his words low, slow and sexy as hell.

Lowrie smiled, lowered her head and placed her lips against his. He allowed her to explore, play, and when she sucked his lower lip between hers, he released the smallest of growls. He lifted his hand to cup the back of her head. Gently tugged on her hair to pull her head back so he could look into her eyes.

"Is that all the game you've got, Lowrie?"

Seeing the challenge in his eyes, she held the side of his face and placed her lips on his, sliding her tongue along the seam. He opened his mouth and she slipped her tongue inside, enjoying the sensation of being in control. It didn't last long because Sutton's grip on her head tightened and, on a low groan, he took over, sweeping her into a passionate kiss that had her head swirling and her heart thumping.

His tongue twirled around hers, and her blood superheated. His thumb brushed over her nipple and her blood started to boil.

She wanted him, of that she had no doubt. No one had ever made her feel so alive, so quickly. He shut down her brain and circumvented her common sense, and she was okay with that, as long he kept kissing her, touching her.

She slid down so that the space between her thighs was flush against his erection and she couldn't help wriggling a little, trying to hit the spot. The world could end, a bomb could detonate, but as long as those apocalyptic events didn't stop her from making love to Sutton on this couch in front of a fire, she didn't care.

Lowrie sighed as his mouth traced the contours of her cheekbone, whispered over her jaw, sighed when his tongue sucked on the delicate flesh between her neck and ear. Impatient, she pulled up his T-shirt, her fingers dancing across his muscled stomach, her thumb brushing through the line of hair that disappeared beneath his pajama pants.

This was sweet madness...

Sutton took her mouth again and she tasted chili and chocolate, tequila and temptation, as she sucked on his tongue, arching her breasts into his hands. Her womb pulsed, her soul whimpered with need and she knew that when he lifted his mouth to allow her to speak, she'd ask him to take her to bed.

In his arms, for the first time in over eighteen months, she felt like a woman. Desirable. Having a delicious man tell her she was hot reminded her that before she was a mother, she was Lowrie.

Before she was a mother...

Something deep inside her, intuition or a mother's sense that something was wrong, had her pulling away from Sutton to cock her head. She looked over to the baby monitor but it was silent.

"Come back here," Sutton told her, reaching up to cup her neck.

She held up a finger… Three, two, one…

Waaah!

Lowrie slammed her eyes shut and tipped back her head to glare up at the ceiling. Her son had awful timing…

Waah, waah, waah.

Right, that was a where-are-you-need-you-right-now wail. He wouldn't settle down and go back to sleep. In fact, she was pretty certain he was climbing to his feet and holding the sides of his crib, tears running down his face.

He was either scared or in pain, possibly both.

Lowrie grimaced and met Sutton's eyes. "Sorry."

He lifted his hands in a what-can-you-do? gesture. Lowrie climbed off him, straightened her pajama top and, out of the corner of her eye, saw him adjusting the fabric of his pants. He sent her a pained smile.

"Babies have the worst timing in the world."

"No problem," Sutton replied. "He's your top priority, I get that." He winced when Rhan turned up the volume. "I can't believe something so small can make so much noise."

She sent him a grateful look before walking over to the baby monitor and picking it up. "I'll see you in the morning."

"Good night, Lowrie."

Feeling frustrated, Lowrie walked toward the hallway. When she reached the stairs, she ran up one flight, then another and walked into her extensive upstairs apartment, and through its open-plan living room. She walked into the smaller of the two rooms and there he was, tears running down his little face. She swung him up, sighed when he buried his face in her neck and patted his little bottom.

"Mommy's here, baby. She'd much rather you were sleeping and she was on the couch with Sutton exploring his delicious body, but she's here. Shhh, baby boy."

Lowrie, for various reasons, got very little sleep that night.

Why was he sent to The Rossi? Why did Benjamin Ryder-White want him here, at this small, lovely place on the outskirts of Portland? What was the connection between Benjamin and this place?

The next morning Sutton stood on the covered porch off his bedroom, his hands jammed into the pockets of his sleeveless parka. It was the first clear day in ages and the air was bitingly cold but bearable. He'd recently returned from an eight-mile run and he needed to get to work, but the urge to take ten minutes to suck in the view couldn't be ignored.

The sea was gunmetal-gray, hinting at violence beneath its surface, and weak sunlight danced on the sand of the small beach between the boulders.

Sutton brushed snow from the balcony railing and leaned his forearms on the wood, his thoughts bouncing from the intensely passionate kiss he'd shared with Lowrie last night to the mystery of his birth father.

It was easier to think of his birth father than it was to think of Lowrie, as he'd already spent half the night reliving what was probably the hottest kiss of his life. He'd been surprised when she'd climbed onto his lap, unable to believe she'd made the first move. But very damn grateful. Her skin felt like silk beneath his hands, her mouth like the ripest, sweetest fruit, and he'd felt the heat of her core beneath their clothes. It had taken everything he had not to strip her down and take her on the carpet in front of the fire...

He was doing it again, giving those few minutes holding her far too much mental energy. Sutton scrubbed his hands over his face and glared at the rocks below.

Move the hell on...

Right, Benjamin Ryder-White.

When he came to Portland, he'd resolved that he was here for one reason and one reason only: the bucks. One hundred and fifty million, to be precise.

The money he was on the brink of inheriting would fund the running costs of the children's home his parents established for yet-to-be-adopted orphans and at-risk kids for a long time, with change to spare. The home had been so important to his parents, and he and Thea had taken their seats on the charity's board when they passed on. Thea with enthusiasm, him with trepidation.

He'd never felt comfortable with the idea of a charity to support orphans; it struck too close to home. Would he have been one of the kids who ended up there, or in the system, had his birth mother not been rich, if she hadn't found the Tate-Handler Agency? Where would he be if his mum had fallen pregnant before they adopted him? He couldn't help imagining that other baby, the one they'd been thinking of adopting when they heard that Thea was on the way… What had happened to him? Or her? Had someone else taken him? Was he raised in a crappy home, or a place like The Marching Ant House?

His parents, God bless them, had high standards for their orphanage, its name a play on their surname. All caregivers were carefully chosen for their kindness and empathy. Young babies and toddlers were given all the attention and love they needed. Small groups of younger children were placed in the care of a foster mother—or father—and that person was their "parent" until they left the facility at eighteen. Teenagers were also matched with older brothers and sisters, people to guide them.

The Marching Ant House was a happy place, but it was only one and there were hundreds, thousands, of kids who weren't raised in such a loving environment. And, yeah, if Benjamin's money could build, establish and fund another two or three houses, that's what Sutton would use it for.

But why The Rossi? Why did he have to stay here for another month and a half?

Why did he care? It. Didn't. Matter.

They'd chosen to give him up; he'd chosen not to find out anything about them.

Simple enough.

Sutton heard a baby laughing and looked down to see Lowrie stepping onto the veranda from the sitting room, little Rhan gripping her finger and toddling beside her. He held a stuffed giraffe beneath his arm and plopped down on the cold floor. Sutton watched, fascinated, as a massive mop of a dog ambled onto the veranda and sat down next to Rhan, laying a gentle paw on the little boy's thigh. Rhan wrapped a handful of the dog's corded fur in his hands, hauled himself up and snuggled into its huge chest. Sutton smiled when the dog's paw snuck behind the boy to hold him in place.

Rhan laughed again, pulled away and toddled off toward the railing. The dog immediately put himself between the boy and the railing, as if to protect him. Rhan couldn't fall through the slats but Sutton was impressed with the dog's strong instinct to guard Lowrie's son.

Lowrie, holding a mug in her hand, praised the dog, gave it a biscuit that she pulled from her jacket pocket and turned to speak to someone inside.

"It's actually lovely outside," she said, her words drifting up to him.

She was lovely, he thought, happy to watch her. She wasn't his usual type —a little too thin, a bit nervy— but God, he'd never been so aware of a woman in all his life. She was…*magnetic* and he couldn't pull his attention off her.

Lowrie had pulled her hair into a ponytail and wore a little makeup this morning, maybe mascara and a peach-colored lipstick. Her long legs were covered in tight, black denims that disappeared into low-heeled, knee-high boots. Her sweater was a cheery red. A cream, sheepskin aviator jacket ended at her shapely hips—hips he'd held in his hands last night.

Two ladies, one a lot older than the other, stepped onto the veranda. Sutton watched as Lowrie took a tray from the younger woman and placed it on the wrought-iron table. Sutton looked down at the tray and saw cinnamon buns, steam rising off them.

Cinnamon buns? Where were his?

Lowrie stepped back into the house for a minute and when she returned, she spread out a thick blanket on the floor next to their chair and tipped out a box of toys for Rhan. He looked at them, ignored them and walked his giraffe along the enormous dog's back.

Lowrie suddenly looked up and their eyes connected, then clashed. She blushed and he grinned, amused by her embarrassment. They were two consenting adults and they hadn't done anything illegal. They'd kissed…

Though that was a very weak description of the way he'd inhaled her, how he'd fought to keep from stripping her naked and plunging inside her.

Sutton took a couple of deep breaths and reminded himself that he wasn't fifteen anymore. When he felt more in control, he spoke. "Can you spare a cinnamon bun?" he asked, resting his arms on the railing.

"Come on down and meet my grandmother and aunt," Lowrie told him, her hands on her hips. "Would you like a cup of coffee?"

"Sure, but I'll make it." He turned to walk away but stopped, thinking of the dog. "If I come down there, will I be attacked by the oversized mop?"

Lowrie's grin was like fireworks exploding in a night sky. "Maybe. How much do you want a cinnamon bun, Marchant?"

Home-baked and still warm? Hell, he'd take his chances.

Five

In between being interrogated about his books—
Lowrie was unaware that her grandmother and aunt
were into crime novels—Sutton ate three of Jojo's famous cinnamon buns and drank two cups of coffee.
He kept a wary eye on Charlie, and Charlie treated
him with supreme indifference.

She wished she could say the same.

Sutton was a difficult guy to ignore, and not just
because he was tall, broad and big. This morning he
wore dark blue Levi's that cupped his butt in the most
delicious way, waterproof boots and an ivory-colored
hoodie. He hadn't shaved—after living with him for
over a week, she realized he wasn't a fan of scrap-
ing his face daily—and his hair was its usual mess.

Supersexy man.

Lowrie sighed, annoyed with herself.

She'd promised herself that she'd be the consummate host this morning, that she'd treat him like any other guest, and she was trying, she really was. But he'd had his tongue in her mouth, his hands had covered her boobs and traced the contours of her ass with immense skill. If Rhan hadn't cried, there was no doubt that she would know what it felt like to be loved by him, to have him slide inside her, rock her to heaven.

Lowrie ran her hand over her eyes, sighing. She wasn't on the pill. Dressed as he was, it was obvious that he hadn't had any condoms on his person and they'd been so into each other that birth control might've been forgotten. It certainly hadn't crossed her mind. With Rex, she'd been dogmatic about taking the pill, but a dose of antibiotics messed with her protection and that's how she got pregnant with Rhan.

But she hadn't been on the pill in ages, so if she and Sutton got it on, they'd need to use condoms. If they got it on… Yeah, her mind, or more likely her needy body, wasn't moving off the possibility.

She wanted him more now, knowing what an excellent kisser he was, how he'd set her body alight with one slide of his hand and a few hot-as-lava kisses.

This wasn't good, this wasn't good at all. He was just another man who'd dropped into her life, and he was only in the country for the next six weeks. He wasn't, she was sure, the type who wanted to stick around.

But she didn't want one of those, did she? She wasn't looking for a man to marry, to help her raise her son, a man to love. She'd loved enough people in her life who'd let her down, so why would she want to add one more to the list?

But sex would be good. Sex with Sutton would be, she was convinced, a mind-bending, soul-touching, body-melting experience.

She just had to let her body have some fun without allowing her heart into the party...

"Don't you think so, Low?"

On hearing her grandmother say her name, her head snapped up. "Sorry, what?"

Jojo's eyes narrowed with speculation. "You haven't listened to a word we've said."

Lowrie tried to recall snippets of their conversation to refute her accusation but came up with nothing. She shrugged, saw Sutton's lips twitch in amusement and glared at him. "Sorry. Miles away."

"I was saying that there's an art exhibition at the Portland Museum of Art. Gavin Price? Wasn't he a friend of yours from New York?"

"No, Mama, Lowrie had an exhibition with him," Isabel corrected.

Sutton's gaze sharpened and Lowrie wrinkled her nose. Her past as an up-and-coming artist wasn't a secret but neither did she blab about it. How did she tell people that art had started making her feel sick, that she'd found herself falling apart under the stress of being one of the country's most exciting painters? That her life collapsed when her agent-fiancé threatened to ditch her at her lowest moment, telling her that he wasn't interested in dealing with children having temper tantrums.

She'd asked for help and got none, and the only way to survive had been to drop out, to disappear. She still associated painting with panic attacks, racing thoughts and feeling out of control. She hadn't picked up a brush or a palette, not even a pencil, in over six years.

She couldn't go back there, to that terrifying place where she was solely judged on the work she produced, the money she made—for her fiancé and her gallery-owning mother—and the reputation she was building.

"You're an artist?" Sutton asked her, his index finger tapping against his coffee mug.

"I *was* an artist," Lowrie replied, mentally grimacing at her short reply.

"Lowrie had a few exhibitions in New York and was regarded as one of the most exciting artists of her generation," Jojo explained, her tone proud. "Of course, art runs in her blood. My brother was an incredible artist, as is my daughter. She owns a gallery in Lenox Hill—Lily Lewis…?"

Since her mom's gallery was one of the most famous in the city, Lowrie wasn't surprised at seeing Sutton's immediate recognition of the name. "Your father is the sculptor Roscoe Lewis."

Lowrie nodded and looked away. She really didn't want to talk about this anymore. She missed her art, missed creating, but she didn't miss feeling panicky or pressured to perform.

"What can you tell me about this house, ladies?" Sutton asked.

Lowrie darted a look his way, grateful to him for changing the subject. He half smiled at her and reached for another cinnamon roll. Was that his fourth? Where did he put all that food? He winked at her as he took a huge bite out of the pastry.

"What do you want to know?" Isabel asked, surprising Lowrie with her question. Her grandmother was feisty, never afraid to speak her mind, but Isabel was a quiet soul and shy around strangers. She hardly ever instigated conversation. It was strange for her to be so at ease with Sutton. Or any man.

Sutton lifted one powerful shoulder in a shrug. "When was it built?"

Jojo jumped in, telling Sutton the history of the hundred-year house, that her grandfather built it and that her brother Carlo inherited it over forty years ago.

Jojo gestured to her. "Carlo didn't have any kids and Lowrie is the only grandchild so it will be hers one day."

Sutton frowned. "I thought Paddy owned it."

"Paddy has the right to live in it until he dies, but it will be Low's, then Rhan's," Jojo insisted. "It's a huge place and it requires upkeep so Carlo and Paddy turned it into an inn twenty years ago."

Sutton swallowed the last of his cinnamon roll and linked his hands across his flat stomach. "I can understand that. My sister and I inherited a house in

Sussex from my parents that's been in the family for hundreds of years and we converted it into a small hotel so it could pay its way. These old houses suck up cash."

Jojo nodded. "Great minds think alike."

Sutton placed his ankle on his opposite knee and played with the laces in his boot. "Lowrie told me you are a fount of knowledge about local families and you follow the local news. What can you tell me about the Ryder-Whites?"

Jojo didn't hesitate. "Kinga Ryder-White is dating Griff O'Hare, the singer. You know, the one who threw a chair through a hotel window in Dubai?" Lowrie shook her head, amazed by the things Jojo remembered. "Good-looking boy, but trouble. All good-looking men are trouble."

Lowrie coughed to cover her laugh and although Sutton's expression didn't change, she saw amusement in those extraordinary eyes.

"Tinsley and her ex-brother-in-law, Cody Gallant, are organizing another event to celebrate a hundred years of Ryder International being in business. James and Penelope Ryder-White—"

"Callum Ryder-White's son and daughter-in-law?" Sutton interrupted.

Jojo nodded. "Right. Well, they attended a fundraising dinner for cancer last week. Very into fundraising is Penelope. She runs the Ryder Foundation."

Thinking that her relatives would get a kick out of knowing that Sutton would be attending the Ryder-White ball later tonight, Lowrie told them the news.

They laughed with delight, clapped their hands together and demanded to know who he was taking—no one—and why he was going, but he dodged that question. They insisted that he take photographs and tell them everything. Everything, you hear.

"And if you want to get Griff O'Hare's autograph, that would be okay, too," Isabel murmured.

Jojo hooted. "Isabel has the biggest crush on Griff O'Hare! She could be his mother, but there it is."

"I've got a crush on him, too, Is," Lowrie told her aunt and it wasn't a lie. O'Hare was one sexy man. "It should be illegal for a man to look that good."

The hell of it was, and she would never admit this, but if given the choice between the bad boy of rock and roll and Sutton, well, the broody man opposite her would win that toss.

Dammit.

"Yeah, yeah…got it," Sutton grumbled. He dropped his leg, sat up and leaned forward. His expression turned intense. "Do either of you know if Benjamin Ryder-White has any connection to this house?"

Jojo's mouth fell open and Isabel released a little squeak. They both, perfectly synchronized, stood up, and Jojo snapped her fingers to call Charlie. "It's time to go," Jojo said, picking up her handbag. "Thanks for coffee, darling Low. Nice to meet you, Sutton."

Sutton looked from Lowrie to their departing backs and back to Lowrie again. "Was it something I said?"

Lowrie sent him a ya-think look and shrugged.

"Good to know that mentioning Benjamin Ryder-White's name will clear the room."

"But why?" Sutton asked.

"Good question," Lowrie said. She scooped up Rhan, placed him on her hip and followed her relatives into the house, determined to find out.

When Lowrie returned, a good forty-five minutes later, she was minus her child. Sutton had moved into the library, built up a fire and was looking at an email of two potential book covers, neither of which he liked.

He glanced up, watching as she went to the fire to warm her hands. It was close to noon and she was normally in the kitchen at this time of day, making food for Rhan and for him.

"No Rhan?" he asked, leaning back in the ergonomic leather office chair he'd had delivered. Yeah, it was pricey, but he was a big guy and he spent a lot of time with his ass plastered to the seat so it was a good investment.

"Jojo and Is kidnapped him for the afternoon, possibly the night," Lowrie told him. "They adore having him and, as much as I love him, it's nice to have a break now and again."

"Did they give you an explanation for their bolting out of the room at me mentioning Benjamin Ryder-White?"

Lowrie shrugged. "I asked, they ignored me. It's weird because they are pretty chatty people."

"Yeah, I gathered, especially your grandmother."

He laid a hand on his heart and tapped it. "If she were forty years younger…"

Lowrie grinned. "I know, right? She's a fire-cracker."

Sutton looked at her, enjoying her wide smile as she talked about her relatives. "But what is a four-foot-nothing Italian nonna doing with a dog the size of a baby cow that looks like an old-fashioned mop?"

Lowrie turned her back to the fire and Sutton wanted to suggest a better way of warming her up but managed to keep that asinine suggestion to himself.

"Isabel found Charlie on the side of the road, a couple of months before Rhan was born. He was just a puppy and they brought him home, not knowing what he was or how big he'd get."

"Apart from being ninety percent mop, what breed is he?"

"He's a Komondor, also known as the Hungarian sheepdog. Quite rare and we have no idea how he came to be lost or abandoned because he's definitely purebred."

"You're very comfortable with him being around your kid."

Lowrie pulled out her phone, flicked through it and walked over to him to show him the screen. He looked at the photo of Charlie, sprawled out, and a newborn Rhan lying between his chest and front leg. Both dog and human were fast asleep.

"I have dozens more. Charlie has been besotted with Rhan from the moment they met. Now that Rhan is becoming more mobile, he's an amazing pair of second eyes."

Yeah, he'd noticed that. Lowrie took back her phone, placed a hand on his shoulder and looked at his big monitor, filled with the two images of the competing book covers.

"Nice," she said, her tone polite.

He shook his head. "Do you think so? I don't know if I like either of them." He stared at the screen and attempted to be casual. "You're an artist, what do you really think?"

Lowrie crossed her arms over her chest, stared at his screen and contemplated the first image. "It's too busy, for one. I'd make the background black and white so it comes across as spookier, more atmospheric. I'd change the white writing to red, maybe have a couple of droplets dripping off the last two letters." She glanced at him. "It does have dead bodies, right?"

"Many," Sutton confirmed. He cocked his head to the side. "I agree with you. I'll send your suggestions back and see what they come up with. Thanks."

"Pleasure," Lowrie said as she sat down behind her messy desk. Their desks faced each other but if he looked left and she right, they both had an exceptional view of the bay.

"I'm going to pay some bills, do some admin," Lowrie told him. "I'll be quiet so as not to disturb you."

"Don't worry about that, I'm done with work today.

I'm going to be leaving for the airport in a couple of hours."

Lowrie nodded. "Right, the Ryder International Ball."

"Mmm." He really wasn't looking forward to it. Spending his evening in a room full of strangers, making small talk, dressed in a penguin suit, wasn't his idea of fun.

"Poor boy, drinking the world's best champagne, eating amazing food, listening to Griff O'Hare sing," Lowrie said, tongue firmly in her cheek.

"He doesn't have quite the same effect on me as he has on you. And Isabel," he muttered, annoyed that he was just a little jealous.

"As I said, talented and hot. It's a killer combination."

Sutton propped his boots on the corner of the desk, leaning back in his chair. He really didn't want to rush off to Manhattan and spend the night in a cold hotel room, but what choice did he have? If he wanted Benjamin's money, it was what he had to do...

But maybe he wouldn't have to spend the entire evening alone. "Come with me."

Lowrie looked up, her expression puzzled. "What?"

"Come with me to New York City," he said. "I've got to make an appearance at this bloody ball but no one said I had to stay for the whole thing. I'll hang around for an hour, maybe two, and then we can go to dinner, walk the streets, ride around Central Park in one of those carriage things."

"They are called hansom cabs," Lowrie replied,

slitting open an envelope to pull out a bill. "And no. But thank you."

"Why not?" Sutton demanded.

Lowrie rolled her eyes. "Well, I have a young son I can't leave—"

"You said that he might stay the night with your grandmother and aunt."

"But I like being close by. They live just down the road and I can be there in under five minutes if there's a problem."

"True enough. But what's going to happen with a guard-dog-slash-babysitter in the house and two very eagle-eyed, doting women?"

She looked tempted. And excited. Then she shook her head. "It's a silly idea, Marchant."

"It's a *great* idea, Lewis. I already have a hotel room booked at the Forrester-Grantham, and my plane is waiting for me at Portland Jetport. My suite has a hot tub and awesome views of Central Park. I'll order you wine and sushi, or anything else you want to eat, and you can kick back in the hot bubbles while I go and meet boring people downstairs. I'll do my thing and then we can spend the rest of the evening exploring Manhattan."

"Sutton, I can't just go to New York on a whim with a man I don't know."

"You know me," Sutton calmly stated, holding her eyes. "You might not know what my favorite color is—mint green, by the way—or what music I like, jazz, but you know that I would never harm you." He smiled to lighten the mood. "Besides, we've been living together for nearly two weeks now."

She didn't look convinced.

"Lowrie, take a break. You're a great mom, and I get that you are worried about leaving Rhan, but he's in amazing hands. Take an evening for yourself—" He looked at his watch. "In fact, if we leave now, we can be there in a couple of hours and we'll have time to do whatever you want to do."

"Would we have time to—" She stopped and waved her hands around. "Don't worry, stupid question."

"Time to do what?"

She lifted her stubborn chin. "It doesn't matter because I'm not going."

Oh, she was thinking about it. "Time to do what, Low?"

She looked out the window and released a little sigh. "Visit the Frick Museum."

He moved his mouse, pulled his keyboard to him and asked the internet when the museum closed. He did some calculations and worked out that if they hustled, they could have two hours at the museum before it closed. That would still give him more than enough time to shower and change and get downstairs to the Forrester-Grantham ballroom.

"We've got time. C'mon, Lowrie, come play with me."

She bit her bottom lip, scratched the back of her neck. "When you say *play*, what, exactly, do you mean by that?"

He saw the flash of vulnerability in her eyes and sighed. He knew what she was asking... How was he expecting to be paid for this unexpected trip? Man, she had to start hanging out with better men.

"There's no quid pro quo here, Lowrie. I'm going to Manhattan, anyway. My sister booked a suite, but if there's no second bed, I'll sleep on the couch. I'm not expecting payment, in any shape or form."

She rubbed her forehead with her fingertips. "I don't know, Sutton."

He stood up and walked over to her desk, placing his hands on its surface and lowering his head so his eyes were level with hers. "Call your grandmother, ask her what she thinks. Find out if she's happy for you to go, happy to look after Rhan, and if she is, come and find me, okay?"

Knowing that if he pushed her further, he might lose her, Sutton left the room, thinking that he had, maybe, a thirty percent chance of her company.

Well, it was still a chance.

In the bathroom of his suite at the Forrester-Grantham Hotel, Sutton threaded cuff links through the buttonholes of his white dress shirt and rubbed his smooth face. The last thing he wanted to do was go downstairs and be sociable, but needs—specifically The Marching Ant's needs—insisted he must.

He'd much rather stay here and slide into that hot tub, preferably naked, with Lowrie. Sutton reached for his toothbrush and paste, thinking about the fun afternoon they'd spent looking at art in the Frick Museum.

Being with her was like having his own personal tour guide, as her knowledge about art history, techniques and design was encyclopedic. She might not have a college degree, but she knew her subject inside out.

She was intelligent, interesting and had a dry sense of humor he found incredibly attractive.

Getting her to spend the evening with him in Manhattan had been difficult—she'd second-guessed her decision to leave Rhan right until the plane took off. When they landed, she checked her phone for messages, called Jojo and immediately offered to catch the first plane home. Jojo insisted Rhan was absolutely fine and that she stay in New York City. He'd be buying Lowrie's grandmother an enormous bouquet of flowers when he returned to Portland.

Lowrie didn't call her grandmother again, but he did see her exchange a number of text messages to check up on Rhan. Her son was everything to her.

Lucky kid.

He'd been lucky, too, but he'd been so wrapped up in his own insecurities, so intent on protecting himself from his parents' unlikely but possible rejection, that he hadn't noticed how involved his parents were in his life. They attended parent-teacher meetings, sports matches. Every evening they gathered around the dinner table and talked about their day, what was happening in their lives. Thea rattled on, telling them everything, but they'd had to pry every nugget of information out of him...

Even back then he'd found opening up difficult.

He was surprised he'd told Lowrie he was adopted;

it wasn't a subject he ever raised. Even more shocking was his desire to tell her the whole story, to blurt out why he was really going to this ball, why he was staying at her inn for the foreseeable future.

He never opened up; it wasn't what he did. He dealt with his issues alone, or on the pages of a book, and never let people into his headspace. He wanted to confide in her and didn't know why.

What was it about the single mom, onetime artist and current innkeeper that drew him like a moth to a flame?

She was…authentic, Sutton decided. She was just trying to win life, not wrapped up in the bullshit of ego or success. She wanted to be a good mom, do a decent job running the inn. She seemed content with her life.

But why had she given up on art? Trailing behind her in the Frick Museum, he'd seen her passion, watched as her eyes sparked with interest, admiration. Noticed how her brow furrowed when she tried to work out how an artist created a particular effect.

He suspected a lot of the art in the inn was hers, and that the massive painting in the hallway was one she'd done years ago. He'd love to see more of her work, and when he had some time, he'd see if he could track down her art.

In the bedroom, Sutton slid his tuxedo jacket off the hanger and walked into the lounge area of the suite. Beyond the massive windows was an impressive view of the city and Lowrie was standing there, a glass of red wine in her hand.

She lifted the glass. "I hope it's okay that I ordered a bottle."

He smiled. "Very." After tossing the jacket over the back of the couch, he walked over to her, plucked her glass out of her hand and took a sip before handing it back to her. "I'm sorry to be leaving you alone tonight," he told her, reaching up to tuck a curl behind her ear.

"It's fine," Lowrie assured him. "Thanks for being patient this afternoon at the museum and sorry if I bombarded you with too much information."

"I enjoyed it," he assured her. He grinned. "And during those few times you stopped talking, I was thinking that a famous, fictional museum would be a perfect place to stage an art theft and a murder."

Her eyebrows raised. "Uh…seriously?"

"Mmm. There would be a table in the dining room where I'd pose a dead body, dripping blood onto a priceless Persian carpet. Obviously, the walls would be stripped of their art. My police detective would be stumped by how the thieves and murderers rearmed the place when they left. Or maybe the murderer used the theft to cover up his crime."

She scratched her forehead. "I was thinking light and technique, and you were thinking dead bodies?"

"It's what I do." Thinking this was the perfect segue into a topic he wanted to raise, he leaned his shoulder against the glass window, his eyes on her lovely face. "Talking of, why don't you paint anymore?"

"How do you know I don't?" Lowrie demanded.

"I've been living with you for nearly two weeks and I haven't smelled paint on you or turpentine. I haven't seen paint on your hands. And I've explored most of the inn and seen no canvases, no easels, no hint of creativity."

Shutters dropped over her eyes, blunting the color. "It's a long story and you're going to be late."

Sutton looked at his watch and grimaced. She was right—if he didn't hustle, he'd be walking in when everyone was seated. He wanted to observe the Ryder-Whites, not bring attention himself.

He played with his yet-to-be-tied bow tie, a little discombobulated by the thought of seeing his blood relatives for the first time ever. Up to this point, the thought of meeting them had been an intellectual exercise, but now it was about to become reality. Would he look like them, talk like them? Would they see the connection? Would he be just another face in the crowd? Probably.

Sutton squared his shoulders, straightened his spine. He was making too big a deal of this. The Ryder-Whites were not his family…

He'd lost half of his family five years ago and they could never be replaced.

"You've turned pale," Lowrie said, putting her hand on his arm. "Are you feeling okay?"

No, unfortunately he felt just the smallest bit sick. But, because he was not someone to show weakness, he pulled up a nothing-to-see-here smile. "Sure, why?"

"Liar," Lowrie told him. She raised her glass, sipped and handed it to him. "I'll make you a deal, Marchant."

"And what might that be?"

"You tell me why you're here in the States, the real reason, and I'll tell you why I don't paint anymore."

It was tempting. He wanted to dig and delve beneath her fake-cool surface but he didn't know if he was ready to tell her, or anyone else, about his birth family and Benjamin's ridiculously enormous bequest. He considered her suggestion. "I'll tell you what I can," he said as a compromise.

Lowrie tipped her head to the side and smiled but didn't say anything.

"No deal?" he asked, disappointed.

"Actually, you gave me more than I expected. You aren't what anyone would call a chatty guy."

He gripped her biceps and stepped closer to her, dropping his head so that his temple rested against the side of her head. "I'm not. But I can ask for what I want."

She angled her head so that her lips were a fraction from his mouth. "And what might that be, Sutton?"

"While I'm gone, will you think about sharing my bed? I can't promise you anything, I don't do relationships, but I promise to make it good for you."

Her lips drifted across his before she pulled away. "I'll think about it," she murmured.

"Fair enough," Sutton replied, kissing her head before stepping back. "I must go. Are you good?"

She raised her glass. "I have wine and I'll order room service when you leave. Then I'm going to hop in that hot tub outside."

"So you brought your bathing suit? I meant to remind you."

The corners of Lowrie's mouth kicked up. "I didn't, actually, but that's not a problem since, despite being on the balcony, the hot tub is quite private."

He closed his eyes at the image of her long, slim and very naked body sliding into the hot bubbles. He started to grow hard and he groaned. "Thanks for that image," he grumbled. "You just shot my concentration to hell, Lowrie."

Lowrie laughed. "It's a ball, Sutton, why on earth do you need to concentrate? Drink some fancy whiskey, eat the amazing food, dance with a pretty girl."

She tugged at one end of his tie, which was lying flat against his chest. "Don't forget about this," she told him.

He couldn't resist brushing his lips against hers. "I wish you were coming with me." He really did—this would be so much easier with her hand in his, her steady gaze grounding him, having someone in his corner.

For a man who was ruthlessly independent, those thoughts scared the crap out of him. So he walked away and did what he always did—thought about something else.

Unfortunately that something else was a naked Lowrie in the hot tub and that made for an extremely uncomfortable trip down to the ballroom.

Six

Sutton watched as Kinga Ryder-White approached their table, the fabric of her red ball gown swishing around her ankles. The brown-eyed blonde—would she be his first or second cousin?—radiated happiness and Sutton knew it had something to do with Griff O'Hare. He had excellent observational skills, but one would have to be clueless not to notice that Kinga and Griff only had eyes for each other.

Isabel would be heartbroken.

Sutton and Garrett Kaye stood up as Kinga approached them and she smiled, before plopping down in the chair his other cousin, Tinsley, had vacated at least an hour before. Neither Tinsley nor Cody Gallant had returned to the ball and Sutton doubted they'd be seeing them again that night. Electricity had arced between them all night, as it had with Garrett Kaye and Kinga's friend, Jules Carson.

Sutton had spent the evening dodging lightning bolts between the potential couples and it was a bloody miracle he'd yet to be electrocuted.

Garrett introduced Kinga to Sutton and when they were all seated again, Kinga rested her chin in the palm of her hand. "Are you guys having fun?" she asked.

"Surprisingly, yes," Garrett said.

Instead of being offended by his blunt reply, Kinga just laughed. "And you, Sutton?"

He said he was and it wasn't a complete lie. He had enjoyed his evening, more than he'd expected to.

"We seated you at this table partly because this is the singles table but mostly because Tinsley and I are huge fans of your work," Kinga told him, smiling.

Sutton thanked her, thinking that he'd enjoyed the company at the table. He'd met Garrett Kaye years ago through Sam—Kaye Capital and MarchBent had done business together— so seeing him sitting at the table was a pleasant surprise.

He instinctively liked Cody Gallant, the owner of an international events company. Jules Carson, a semifamous mixologist, was both lovely and funny, and he'd found Tinsley quietly charming.

Kinga radiated soul-deep happiness. Good for her.

Kinga ordered a glass of champagne from a passing waiter and looked toward the empty stage. She glanced at the diamond bracelet watch on her left wrist and released a quiet sigh.

"Long night?" Sutton asked her.

She smiled and he saw the exhaustion in her eyes. "Honestly, it's been a long year. I can't wait until this evening is over and I can sleep for a week."

Sutton looked around the exquisitely decorated ballroom, recognizing a German princess and a European industrialist. A Danish politician was talking to an Arab sheikh and two A-list celebrities—not married to each other—were making out on the dance floor. The ball had most definitely lived up to its hype and Sutton was impressed. "You and your sister did an impressive job, Kinga."

Kinga's smile was tired but appreciative. "Thank you. Oh, God…"

Garrett raised his eyebrows. "Problem?"

She shook her head. "My grandfather is bearing down on us, with an I-need-to-talk-to-you look on his face." Trepidation shimmered in her eyes and Sutton felt his protective instincts rise.

Callum Ryder-White—tall, stooped and flint-eyed – approached them, his son James two steps behind him. Sutton noticed the long look James exchanged with his daughter, and had he not been looking so closely, would've missed the small shake of James's head.

Right, things were about to get interesting, Sutton thought, climbing to his feet again.

Kinga introduced him to Callum and James, while Garrett stood back, his expression sardonic. It seemed Sutton wasn't the only one who had issues with the Ryder-White men.

"Welcome to my ball, gentlemen," Callum said in his raspy voice.

His ball? From what he'd gathered, Callum's granddaughters had worked their tails off to create the event and his daughter-in-law was the powerhouse behind the Ryder Foundation. The old man had no problem claiming credit he wasn't due.

"And what's your line of work?" Callum asked Sutton, his tone just the wrong side of bored.

If he wanted to impress him, Sutton could disclose he held a minor royal title, was the co-owner of a property that had been in his family for over four hundred years, had a degree from Oxford and was the founder of an exceptionally lucrative and very respected investment firm.

But because he was contrary, and instinctively didn't like this man—his uncle—he slowly smiled. "Oh, I write blood books."

Callum's already frosty eyes narrowed. "Blood books?"

"Sutton is an international bestselling author of crime novels, Callum," James informed him, smoothing over the awkward moment. Sutton suspected he did a lot of that.

"So you just play with words?"

Play? He wished. Sutton shrugged, not bothering to explain the long hours, frustration and sheer bloody hard work entertaining readers entailed.

Callum harrumphed—huh, Sutton had never actually heard someone do that before—and turned away to look at Garrett Kaye. Sutton saw the amusement in Kinga's eyes and winked. She coughed to cover her giggle.

"Mr. Kaye, I hear that you have an exceptional hacker on your staff."

Beside him, every inch of Garrett's massive frame tensed. "You heard wrong, Mr. Ryder-White."

Callum frowned at him. "But Emma said—"

"My mother misunderstood, sir."

Garrett's voice suggested that Callum not argue, and Callum, obviously not used to being shut down, lifted his nose in the air and stalked off. They watched him go and when he was out of earshot, Garrett looked at James. "I would suggest that you inform your father that openly seeking a hacker might make certain regulatory bodies, like the goddamn police, start looking his way."

James briefly closed his eyes and shook his head. "I swear he's losing it. And what the hell is Emma thinking, passing along that sort of information?"

Kinga nudged Sutton's arm with her elbow. "Garrett's mother is Callum's longtime personal assistant."

Right, that explained why Callum felt comfortable asking Garrett about a hacker. Obviously, he just thought Sutton was an idiot and beneath his notice.

Garrett asked the burning question Sutton himself had been dying to know. "What does Callum need a hacker for?"

James and Kinga exchanged a long look before James shrugged. "It's public knowledge that a quarter of Ryder International's shares, shares that were originally owned by his younger brother Benjamin, are held by an outside party—"

Do not react, dammit, and do not *draw attention to yourself.*

"Callum has been obsessed by those shares for decades and he wants to own them, to keep the bulk of RI stock under family control."

"And by family, my dad means under Callum's control," Kinga muttered.

Wow. Callum Ryder-White wasn't a popular guy. Sutton couldn't understand why, since the man had *such* a sparkly personality.

"So find the owner and make him an offer," Sutton suggested, deliberately sounding obtuse.

James, to his credit, just smiled at his exceptionally naive statement. "His identity has been hidden from us in a trust and we can't access it. I presume that's why Callum is talking about hacking." James ran his hand around the back of his neck, obviously agitated.

"Well, I suggest you talk him out of it, James," Garrett said, his voice hard. "Prison orange is not his color."

James nodded and turned away, taking Kinga with him. Garrett rubbed his hand over his lower jaw and watched them go. "I need a whiskey," he told Sutton. "You coming?"

"Yeah." Not because he needed a drink but because he needed to know whatever Garrett Kaye knew about the Ryder-Whites. Sutton knew that if Old Man Ryder-White was so desperate to hire a hacker to find out who owned his shares—Benjamin's shares—Sutton was running out of time. If Callum got hold of his name and launched some sort of court application to have Ben's will declared invalid, Sutton could be tied up in legal problems for years, possibly a decade or more. It didn't matter whether the case was legitimate or not—sometimes just having pots of money was enough. If the lawyers found a cash cow, they'd keep finding reasons to milk it.

Sutton had seen enough to know how long it took legal challenges, especially ones of an international nature, to make their way through the courts. If he didn't get Ben's money soon and sell the shares, his parents' charities would not see any money for a long, long time.

Not happening. Not on his watch.

Lowrie looked at her watch—it was past eleven. Sutton had been at the ball for three hours, which meant he would be back soon. That meant she had to decide whether to sleep with the man or not.

She wanted to—he was a great-looking guy, fit and sexy. He kissed like a dream and if he brought the same skills to the bedroom, he'd more than exceed his promise to make it good for her.

She had no fears about whether she'd have a fun time, but she did worry about the potential emotional fallout.

She was going to be all but living with the guy for the next six or so weeks, and if he got bored of her, or bored of sleeping with her, how would they be able to face each other across the breakfast table? How would she be able to treat him like another guest?

But how could she pass up this opportunity to be the spontaneous person she missed being? While she hadn't slept around, she'd dated extensively, got a little hot and heavy with a few guys. Did she want to sleep with Sutton because he made her feel more open, less anxious and way more adventurous than she normally was?

When she was with him, she was reminded of the woman she used to be. She missed that version of herself.

You're overthinking this, Lewis.

Sex with Sutton would be a step out of time, an escape from her day-to-day routine. And sure, knowing that Sutton wanted her was a balm to her shaky self-confidence, reminding her that she was a woman and not just Rhan's mom and Paddy's innkeeper. Just hearing his request had lit a small fire in her stomach, telling her she was desirable and attractive.

Hooking up with Sutton would be a lovely, light, superficial connection. All good things…so why was she still hemming and hawing?

Since Rhan's birth and returning to Portland, she hadn't met many men—or any she wanted to date— and she'd been too busy with Rhan and the inn to go out. She could've embraced technology and registered on one of the popular dating apps, but she didn't have the time or energy to wade through the stalkers and the weirdos to find a connection with someone decent.

And, yes, maybe she had been hiding out, because it was too painful and risky to emotionally connect. She couldn't handle it—after being rejected by her mom, her fiancé and Rex—to love and be left again.

With Sutton, she knew he wasn't looking for more than a hookup—he'd told her exactly that—so she'd be a fool if she wanted more from him than he could give. But could she remain emotionally distant while handing him her body?

Was she going to regret this in the morning? Would her heart start misbehaving and start thinking of happy-ever-after, tossing out how-can-we-make-this-work? questions?

Lowrie heard the door to the room opening, heard him place the key card and his phone on the hallway table. By the time he appeared in the doorway of the living room, his tie was pulled loose and he'd shed his jacket. His hair was messy from running his hand through it and his mouth was tight with tension.

So the ball hadn't been fun. "Hi," she murmured from her position curled up in the corner of the couch.

Sutton's head spun around in the direction of her voice. "Hey."

In the light of the hallway, he navigated his way over to her and sat on the edge of the couch, his thigh pressing into her hip. "Why are you sitting in the dark?"

"Thinking," Lowrie replied.

"About?" When she didn't answer, he laid a hand on her thigh and squeezed. "Everything okay at home? Is Rhan okay?"

She so appreciated him thinking of her baby boy. "He's absolutely fine. No, I was thinking about what answer I'd give you when you walked in here."

His hand tightened on her thigh. "No pressure, Low. I hope you know that?"

"I do," Lowrie replied. She lifted her hand and her fingers drifted down his jaw. "Tough evening?"

He half shrugged. "Not as bad as I expected, actually. Food was good, Griff O'Hare, your idol, was fantastic, I met the Ryder-Whites."

"And what do you think about Portland's first family?" Lowrie asked.

He tipped his head back, thinking. "Callum is a prick. James is, I think, a nice guy and the family peacemaker. I didn't meet his wife, Penelope. The princesses weren't half as snotty as I expected them to be," Sutton replied, his hand stroking her thigh from hip to knee. "I sat with Tinsley Ryder-White and Cody Gallant, Garrett Kaye and Jules Carson—she's a mixologist."

Lowrie nodded. "I follow her on Instagram. She's very beautiful."

"Yet my mind was full of the woman I left upstairs, and I kept looking at my watch, wishing I could leave and come back up here to be with her," Sutton said, his deep voice lower than usual. He dragged the tip of his index finger between the lapels of her oversize robe. "I'd hoped to catch you in the hot tub."

"Would you have joined me?" Lowrie asked him, her tone flirty.

"If you asked me to," Sutton replied.

Claim up to FOUR NEW BOOKS & TWO MYSTERY GIFTS – absolutely FREE!

Dear Reader,

We both know life can be difficult at times. That's why it's important to treat yourself so you can relax and recharge once in a while.

And I'd like to help you do this by sending you this amazing offer of up to FOUR brand new full length FREE BOOKS that WE pay for.

This is everything I have ready to send to you right now:

Try **Harlequin® Desire** books featuring the worlds of the American elite with juicy plot twists, delicious sensuality and intriguing scandal.

Try **Harlequin Presents® Larger-Print** books featuring the glamorous lives of royals and billionaires in a world of exotic locations, where passion knows no bounds.

Or **TRY BOTH!**

All we ask in return is that you answer 4 simple questions on the attached Treat Yourself survey. You'll get **Two Free Books** and **Two Mystery Gifts** from each series you try, *altogether worth over $20*! Who could pass up a deal like that?

Sincerely,

Pam Powers

Harlequin Reader Service

Treat Yourself to Free Books and Free Gifts.

Answer 4 fun questions and get rewarded.

	YES	NO
1. I LOVE reading a good book.	○	○
2. I indulge and "treat" myself often.	○	○
3. I love getting FREE things.	○	○
4. Reading is one of my favorite activities.	○	○

TREAT YOURSELF • Pick your 2 Free Books...

Yes! Please send me my Free Books from each series I select and Free Mystery Gifts. I understand that I am under no obligation to buy anything, as explained on the back of this card.

Which do you prefer?

❏ **Harlequin Desire®** 225/326 HDL GRAN
❏ **Harlequin Presents® Larger-Print** 176/376 HDL GRAN
❏ **Try Both** 225/326 & 176/376 HDL GRAY

FIRST NAME   LAST NAME

ADDRESS

APT.#   CITY

STATE/PROV.   ZIP/POSTAL CODE

EMAIL ❏ Please check this box if you would like to receive newsletters and promotional emails from Harlequin Enterprises ULC and its affiliates. You can unsubscribe anytime.

HD/HP-520-TY22

▲ If offer card is missing write to: Harlequin Reader Service, P.O. Box 1341, Buffalo, NY 14240-8571 or visit www.ReaderService.com ▲

FIRST-CLASS MAIL   PERMIT NO. 717   BUFFALO, NY

BUSINESS REPLY MAIL

POSTAGE WILL BE PAID BY ADDRESSEE

HARLEQUIN READER SERVICE
PO BOX 1341
BUFFALO NY 14240-8571

NO POSTAGE
NECESSARY
IF MAILED
IN THE
UNITED STATES

This was it…do or die. Ask or don't. *Step forward or step back, Lewis?* She might regret sleeping with him in the morning, but there was a damn good chance that she'd regret *not* sleeping with him more.

One night, just one night of being loved by him. Then they'd go back to normal. She suspected— *knew*—she wouldn't, but she was more than happy to ignore that insistent voice.

"A fun night? No strings?" She'd forced the words up her tight throat, over her lips.

Sutton's light eyes darkened with lust. "Yeah."

Lowrie scooted past him and stood up. Looking down at him, she undid the sash and allowed the sides of her robe to fall open, giving him a hint of her shadowed curves and dips. His eyes wandered down her body, a slight smile hitting his lips when he noticed the small tattoo on her ankle.

He surprised her by bending down to lift her foot onto his knee. Embarrassed at what he could see— pretty much everything—she gathered the lapels together and ignored his quirking lips. But instead of speaking, he ran a finger over her brightly colored tattoo.

"Why a sunflower?" he asked.

"It's a happy flower, always looking for the sun," Lowrie replied.

"Got any others?" Sutton asked, his hand running up the back of her calf.

"Underneath my right breast, on my hip."

"Can I see them?" Sutton asked, lowering her foot to the floor.

He was looking at her like she was Édouard Manet's *Olympia*, Gustav Klimt's Adele Bloch, Andy Warhol's blue Marilyn Monroe. She was the *Mona Lisa*, Venus, every stunning woman painted in oils or watercolors on canvas or vellum. Desired, made to feel beautiful.

The admiration in his eyes gave her the courage to push the robe off her shoulders so that it hung behind her back and off her arms, exposing her to his gaze. She turned slightly, allowing him to see a delicate rose on her ribs, mimicking the curve of her right breast. She then pulled the robe aside to show him the teeny-tiny bee on her left hip.

"For me, the more inconspicuous the tattoo is, the sexier it is. It's like I've been allowed in on a very private secret," Sutton told her, his hands coming to rest on her bare hips. He pulled her toward him and laid his lips on her skin, just above her belly button.

"Got any of your own you want to share?" Lowrie asked, pushing her hand into his soft hair.

Sutton looked up at her and grimaced. "I'd love to get a couple but I'm dead scared of needles."

Lowrie laughed. "It's not that painful."

"That's what everyone says, but the one time I made it to the tattoo artist's chair, I nearly punched him when he lifted the gun," Sutton confessed, moving his lips to kiss her little bee. "So sexy."

Lowrie looked down at his bent head, not quite able to believe that she was standing in front of him, all but naked. In fact, there was no point to the robe anymore, so she allowed it to drop to the floor. She fought the urge to cover her breasts, her groin, feeling vulnerable while he was still dressed.

Sutton stood up, clasped her face in his hands and brushed his lips across her mouth in a kiss that was as tender as it was sweet. "I'm a wordsmith but I can't tell you how much I want you, Low, how much I need you."

She held his wrists, sighing as his tongue slid inside her mouth. Ribbons of pure pleasure, hot and sweet, ran down her spine, into her nerves, across her body. Needing to touch him, to feel that glorious skin under the palm of her hands, she tugged his shirt from the waistband of his pants and slid her hands under the hem to touch his hard stomach, to dance her fingers against his ribs.

Growling with frustration, Sutton stepped back and grabbed the back of his shirt by its collar and pulled it over his head, then tossed it away. He toed off his shoes, bent down to pull off his socks and, not giving her a word of warning, swept her up and held her against his chest.

"Bedroom?" she asked breathlessly.

"Eventually," Sutton replied. "We're taking a detour first."

Sutton, still holding her, stepped into the hot tub in his suit pants and gently lowered her into the water, the bubbles popping around her. Sitting on the step, he turned her to face him, pulling her knees so that they rested on either side of his hips.

He wanted to remove his pants—of course, he

did—but for the first time since his teens, he didn't know if he could stop himself from plunging inside her, losing control.

Lifting wet hands, he smoothed her hair back from her face, taking in her fine features, her flushed-with-anticipation skin, her take-me-now eyes.

"You are so very lovely, Lowrie," Sutton told her, tracing her feminine shoulder with his big hand.

She dropped her head to place an openmouthed kiss on his shoulder. "You're not too bad yourself, Sutton," Lowrie told him, her hand trailing down his stomach to find the snap of his pants. After fumbling briefly, she unhooked the tab, eased down the zipper and burrowed her hand under his briefs to find him, hot and heavy and needing her touch. She wrapped her fingers around his erection and smiled. "And so, I have to say, is this."

Unable to speak with her hand on him, Sutton ducked his head to close his lips over her nipple, sucking the perfect bud into his mouth. Through the chlorinated water, he could smell the perfume on her skin. Her hand gripped his head, holding him in place as he pleasured her. Needing no barriers between them, he released her and shoved his hands under his briefs, then pushed them and his trousers down his hips, tossing the wet fabric over the side of the hot tub. Water sloshed onto the floor but he didn't care.

Sutton pulled her into him, and her core hit his, hot and wet and indescribably wonderful. She wrapped her arms around his neck, took his mouth in a hot, openmouthed kiss and rubbed herself on him, using his shaft to pleasure herself. While he had no problem with being used like this, he had a better way to bring her to orgasm.

Using his bulk and strength, he gripped her hips and easily lifted her so that she sat on the edge of the tub, her damp hair streaming down her chest, over her breasts. She shivered.

"Too cold?" he asked, watching goose bumps pebble her skin.

"I'm sure you have an idea of how to warm me up," Lowrie said, looking down at him.

"I do, indeed." He picked up her hands, told her to grip the edge of the tub and then slowly spread her knees. He looked down at her thin strip of hair, her plump feminine lips, and sighed. So pretty.

He dragged his finger down that narrow strip, watching her eyes deepen with intense pleasure as he slipped his finger between her folds and found her button. She released a tiny scream and she tipped back her head, panting softly.

Her skin was flushed, her breaths were irregular, and despite not spending a lot of time pleasuring her, he knew she was close to coming.

He'd use his mouth later, he thought. This first time he wanted to watch as her orgasm hit her, wanted to see the pleasure he gave her.

He reached up with one hand to play with her nipples then slid two fingers into her channel and placed his thumb on her clit. Lowrie screamed again and ground down on his fingers, looking fierce and wild and wonderful.

He was throbbing, his cock aching, but he'd wait, he needed to wait. This was too lovely to miss.

Lowrie put her arms behind her head, her spine arching, lifting her breasts. She held herself there, lovely and luscious while his fingers worked her. His thumb brushed her clitoris again and he felt her shudder, her channel throbbing against his fingers as the waves of her intense orgasm crashed over her.

She sobbed, covered her eyes, bore down again and he felt her come again, not as strong this time but good enough to make her gasp.

She was the most beautiful thing he'd ever laid eyes on. And the memory of her losing control, the lights of the city blazing behind her, would always be etched into his memory.

Sutton pulled his hand away and reached up to pull her back into the water. She sighed when her body hit the heat, her eyes closed as she buried her face in his neck. "Wow."

"Good?" Sutton asked, incredibly pleased by her one-word statement.

"No…amazing," Lowrie said, leaning back and wrapping her long legs around his hips. "But I think you should take me to bed, Sutt. And if you don't have condoms, I might scream."

He brushed strands of damp hair off her face. "I have condoms. And you very definitely are going to scream."

Seven

In Lenox Hill, Lowrie placed her hand on Sutton's
arm, tugging him to a stop on the sidewalk. Standing at the bottom of a set of concrete steps leading up
to an ornate black door, she took in the discreet sign.
What was she doing here? Why was she returning to
the one place she said she never would?

Because, lying in Sutton's arms last night, after
two bouts of truly exceptional lovemaking—Sutton
had exceeded his promise to make it good for her—
she'd thought about being back in New York City
and how that made her feel. Honestly, not as bad as
she'd expected.

She'd always believed that returning to the city
would make her anxious, but she'd yet to feel that
way. Maybe it was the fact that she was older, a little

wiser and had different priorities now, but the thought of being back in the city she'd once called home didn't send her spiraling.

And while she was feeling strong, maybe it was time to exorcise a couple of ghosts.

The sign was new: Lily Lewis Gallery. Opening hours 10:00 a.m to 6:00 p.m. She checked her watch and saw that it was five minutes after ten. She and Sutton could be in and out in thirty minutes, and her mother, who never graced the gallery before noon, would never know she was here.

She didn't know if she'd ever paint again, but in this building were ghosts she needed to put to rest.

Biting her bottom lip, Lowrie walked up the steps, yanked open the door and stepped into the vestibule of the gallery. Taking a deep breath, she pushed through the next door and stepped into the double volume room, the low heels of her boots tapping against the laminated wood floors.

She felt Sutton's bulk behind her and appreciated his hand on her lower back, grounding her. A terribly thin, terribly haughty woman walked over to them, dressed in black, her long hair pulled into a bun. Her mother wore brightly colored couture, but her assistants, she decreed, were to wear black.

"Can I help you?" the woman asked, looking down her rather long nose at Lowrie.

Lowrie smiled, wondering how she'd react if she told the woman that she was Lily's daughter and the artist who'd catapulted this gallery into being one of the city's best.

"We'd just like to look around," Lowrie told her.

The assistant turned to Sutton, that red mouth curling into a come-to-me-baby smile. "Let me know if I can help you with anything."

Lowrie was very sure that she would've gotten the cold shoulder if she'd wandered in here on her own.

After shrugging out of their coats, they draped them over their arms and Lowrie led them into the main viewing space, the center of which was dominated by a series of abstract sculptures. She recognized the work immediately. The figures were her father's and they were stunning.

Sutton looked at the plaque with the artist's details and sent Lowrie a look. "Your dad is incredibly talented."

She couldn't argue with that statement, he really was. "My mom is also an artist—no doubt we'll come across a few of her paintings—and she also owns this gallery."

"I gathered that." Sutton captured her hand in his and raised her knuckles to his mouth. "You're looking a little pale. Are you okay?"

Lowrie shrugged. "Trying not to let memories and ghosts swamp me."

Sutton wrapped his arm around her waist and pulled her into his side. She leaned into his strength, his solidity. "Must've been hard trying to live up to two successful artists in the family."

She released a low, bitter laugh. "Trust me, it was harder to outstrip them in talent and selling power."

She felt Sutton tense, heard his sharp intake of

breath. She lifted her head to look at him, her chin lifting at the shock in his eyes. "My grandmother mentioned my talents but I'm pretty sure you thought she was exaggerating, as any doting grandmother would."

"For about seven years, between the ages of sixteen and twenty-three, I was an art sensation," she explained. "Hard to believe, right?"

Sutton rubbed his hand over his lower jaw, scratchy with stubble. She knew it was scratchy because he'd rubbed it against various parts of her body earlier, and in the most delightful way.

"Not really. I know I've only seen one painting of yours, but it's amazing."

"I did that when I was fourteen and gave it to my uncle Carlo for Christmas."

Sutton's eyes widened. "Fourteen? You painted that at fourteen?"

"I was precocious," Lowrie told him. "I thought I was so sophisticated, painting him a naked lady for his bedroom. I wanted to shock the establishment and I thought it was sexy, which it isn't. Anyway, I was mortified when Jojo pulled me aside and ever so gently told me he was gay."

Sutton's lips twitched with amusement. "It's still an incredible painting, but I don't understand why you don't paint anymore."

"That's a long story and not one I want to get into right now," Lowrie told him, sliding her hand into his and leading him deeper into the gallery. "Let's look at art."

She was grateful that he didn't push her for information, or demand to know why they were here and why she'd turned her back on the art world. Lowrie stopped in front of a mammoth oil, ten feet high and at least fourteen wide, surprised at the relatively realistic view of the New York skyline from the Brooklyn Bridge. The painting leaned into being an abstract but the view was instantly recognizable and the colors equally realistic. It was safe and, dare she say, boring.

Sutton cocked his head to the side. "Do you like it?" he asked.

She wrinkled her nose and pulled a face when she saw the price tag. "At fifty thousand I should, but I don't."

"The artist is going to be an incredibly big name in the art world in a couple of years and it's a solid investment."

The raspy words had Lowrie spinning around. In the doorway to the space marked Staff Only, she saw her mother, dressed in a tangerine-colored suit and skyscraper heels, blond hair immaculately coiffed. She didn't look a day older than she'd looked the last time she'd seen her, six years ago in this very space.

"Lowrie?"

Lowrie stepped closer to Sutton, and reached for him, feeling calmer when his big hand encircled hers. "Hello, Mom."

"What the hell are you doing here?"

Such a gracious welcome!

Lowrie shrugged. "This is Sutton Marchant. Sutton, my mom, Lily Lewis."

Thankfully Sutton didn't release her hand to shake Lily's. Lily barely acknowledged Sutton's existence. "Unless you have at least twenty works ready for exhibition, you're not welcome here, Lowrie."

"I told you that I'd never exhibit again, Mother." Lowrie's voice, to her horror, was thin and insubstantial.

"Then we have nothing to say to each other," Lily told her, her eyes granite-hard.

"Oh, I can think of a few topics of discussion. You could ask about your grandson, your mom, your sister," Lowrie stated, gripping Sutton's hand, hanging on.

"They chose their side."

"Rhan is a year old, Mom, he doesn't take *sides*," Lowrie said, furious at the burning sensation in her eyes. She blinked it away and sucked in a hard breath. "How's Dad?"

Lily gestured to the sculptures behind them. "Working, busy, creative, productive."

Unlike you...

Lowrie heard the unspoken words. *Yeah, got it, Mom, I'm not forgiven. Never will be.*

Lowrie turned her back on her mom and looked at Sutton, whose eyes were flashing with annoyance. The man was pissed, but Lowrie knew his anger wasn't directed at her. He opened his mouth to speak but Lowrie squeezed his hand, begging him not to rush to her defense. Apart from the fact that she didn't need him to fight her battles, her mom was never going to change. There was no point in wasting his words or his energy.

The fact that he wanted to protect her was enough.

God, it felt amazing to have someone standing in her corner. "Let's go, Sutt."

Sutton stroked his thumb across her knuckles. "In a moment," he said. He turned to look at another, quite small painting on the wall at right angles to where they stood. "Is that a Cordyn?" he casually asked Lily.

Her mom straightened. "It is. Do you know his work?"

"I have a couple of his pieces hanging in my home in Knightsbridge."

Knightsbridge, one of the most expensive suburbs in the world. It wasn't like Sutton to name-drop so what was he doing?

"You own a Cordyn?" Lily asked, sounding doubtful.

"I do. I own *Darkness Approaches* and *Darkness Within My Soul*." Sutton pulled his hand from hers and walked to the painting to look at its inscription. "This is *Darkness Before the Dawn*, the third in the series."

Lily's eyes sparked with greed and her lips curled into her salesperson smile. "It was the last painting he did before he died. I acquired it from his wife a few weeks after his funeral." Lily stepped up to join Sutton in front of the painting, Lowrie forgotten. She folded her arms and glared at their backs and reminded herself to be an adult. Sutton was allowed to buy a painting from her mother…

"It's for sale for two hundred thousand dollars," Lily told him. "But since you're a friend of Lowrie's, I'll give you a two-and-a-half-percent discount on that price."

"Don't involve me in your horse-trading," Lowrie muttered.

Sutton looked over Lily's head to wink at her. "That's a kind offer, but…no. I'd rather not purchase from you."

Lowrie couldn't help her wide grin.

"But, but…" Lily spluttered. She waved at the painting. "It's the final in the set! You might never get a chance to buy it again!"

Sutton shrugged. "Then I don't get the chance to buy it again. It's a painting, not a lifesaving kidney." He held out his hand to Lowrie. "Shall we go? I think there's a little boy back in Portland who's missing his mama."

Lowrie placed one hand on her heart, the other in his hand, and sighed. He'd stood up to her mother, walked away from a painting he liked…for *her*. She had to be careful or else she could fall for this man, fall hard.

She just hoped she could stop her heart from doing something that would hurt like hell later.

Sutton led her across the gallery floor toward the front door, pulled it open and gestured for her to precede him. On the steps, in the frigid New York air, they pulled on their coats and wrapped scarves around their throats.

"'Do you really have the other two paintings by Cordyn?" she asked as they hit the pavement.

Sutton nodded to the coffee shop across the street. "Do we have time for coffee or are you desperate to get back to Portland and Rhan?"

She wanted to be with Rhan, that was natural. But she also, selfishly, wanted a little more one-on-one time with Sutton. Surely she could take another couple of hours before rushing back? "Coffee sounds great."

"Well?" she asked after Sutton ordered and they were seated at a small table. "The paintings?"

"I do own them."

Lowrie lifted her hand to her mouth in shock. "I thought you were bluffing!"

He shook his head. "Nope. They hang on my bedroom wall and you can see the progression of light in the paintings. The third would complete the story."

Lowrie reached across the table to grip his hand. "Go and buy it if you want to, Sutt. Please. Don't miss out on the opportunity to own the third painting because of me."

Sutton shook his head, looking obstinate. "As I said, it's just a painting, Lowrie. And I refuse to pad the pockets of a woman who treats her daughter like crap."

So sweet but horribly misguided. "They were just words, Sutton. I've heard worse from her over the years."

His expression darkened. Right, he definitely wasn't going to buy the Cordyn now. Dammit. She hated the idea that he'd lost out on something he'd been looking for because of her.

"Why?"

Lowrie raised her eyebrows. "Why what?"

"Why does she treat you like shit?" Sutton demanded, impatient.

"Ah...that." Lowrie wrinkled her nose and tapped her index finger on the glass table. She looked down, saw that her legs were intertwined with Sutton's beneath the table and liked seeing them like that. It felt...right.

Don't go there, Lowrie.

"Talk to me, Low."

"I don't know how to explain without sounding like I'm blowing my own trumpet," Lowrie said, her voice hesitant.

"Blow away," Sutton said, leaning back so the waitress could place his coffee in front of him. Lowrie smiled her thanks and picked up her teaspoon, dunking it in the frothy milk.

"My parents are good artists, very good, but I am...better." She saw his skeptical expression and rubbed the back of her neck. "Honestly? I was very talented."

"One of the best artists of your generation..." Sutton murmured, repeating Jojo's words.

"So it was said. My dad encouraged me, but the older I got, the less my mom could handle it. I was offered my first exhibition when I was fourteen by a small gallery in SoHo and I sold out. I raked in a ton of money that night. And that's why my mom opened her gallery... That way, she could not only control the sale of my work but she could earn off it as well."

Sutton locked his eyes on hers, his attention completely focused on her.

"In public, she talked me up, but in private she mocked my work, told me I was riding on her and my father's coattails, that it was derivative and that it helped, immeasurably, that I was pretty."

"And your dad?"

"He's a quiet guy, soft, you know? He hated us arguing so he retreated to his studio and left us to fight. Then he moved out to an artist's colony in Arizona and I haven't seen much of him since my late teens."

Anger flickered in his eyes, but he didn't speak and for that Lowrie was grateful.

"I had another show at seventeen, but I started garnering real attention when I exhibited at my mom's gallery in Chelsea shortly after my eighteenth birthday. I had a show every six months for the next six years, and my mom moved her gallery three times on the back of my shows, ending up there." She nodded to the building across the street.

"So she did well off you," Sutton murmured.

"She did *very* well off me and as my star rose, so did hers. She started attracting bigger names. She's now regarded as one of the most powerful gallery owners in the city."

"I still don't understand how you came to give up

something you were incredibly good at," Sutton said, wrapping his big hand around his mug of coffee.

"My mother hired a business manager to look after my money and, God, I was earning a ton of it. Together, they controlled pretty much everything I did, what I earned, where I invested the money… I got an allowance."

"You got an allowance?"

She nodded. "Kyle, my business manager, paid all my living expenses, but if I wanted spending money, I had to ask for it." She shrugged, thinking that sometimes it felt like years ago, other days it felt like yesterday. "I was young and I wanted to please them, but I also wanted to paint and not be bothered, so him paying the bills felt right. But they pushed me to paint more and more, to keep the money rolling in, so that's what I did. I worked, all the time."

"That sounds a little like forced labor," Sutton said, anger in his eyes.

"I did, eventually, start to rebel, telling them that I needed to get out, to party, to have a life. So Kyle and my mom concocted a plan to give me what I wanted. Kyle started taking me out, to parties and shows, flirting with me and treating me like a princess.

"I was pretty sheltered and overprotected and I hadn't had a boyfriend so I loved the attention I received from him. He was older and charming and sophisticated, and he made me feel amazing."

Sutton winced. "And after a great night out, he'd push you back into your studio and tell you to paint?"

Basically. She nodded. "I thought I was in love, but

every year I became unhappier. Kyle proposed, I accepted and I thought that would make me happy, but it didn't. I'd paint and party with him, with his friends, attending all these celebrity events with artists and creatives and movers and shakers. And I hated every minute. I hated the art I was doing, I thought I was rubbish and I lost control of my stress levels."

"What did you do?" Sutton asked.

"I asked for help, I didn't get it. I told them I wanted to change direction, they talked me out of it. I couldn't sleep, barely ate, and I would randomly start crying while I was working. I was constantly terrified of letting them down or having them not love me if I didn't give them what they wanted. Their opinions meant everything. Because they kept telling me that they didn't understand the hype around me, that I was a fad that would fade away, that I needed to milk my fame while I remained in the public eye, I kept working at a frenetic pace."

She released a long breath before continuing. "But the quality of my work dropped and my heart wasn't in what I was painting. At times I felt I was going insane, my mind raced constantly and I kept imagining running away." She'd never told anyone, not even Rex, this much about her past... God, did her son's father even know that she was once a semifamous painter? She didn't think their conversations had ever gone that deep. And how sad was that?

"So what was the final straw, Lowrie?" Sutton asked, leaning forward.

"It was the opening night of my newest show, in

that very room we were just in. I arrived late and Kyle criticized my outfit in front of a bunch of art critics, and my mom agreed with him. I felt something crack inside me and I went to the bar and tossed back a tequila shot. Then another."

Sutton winced and she nodded. "Yeah, not clever. I wasn't drunk, but I did become uninhibited."

"What did you do?"

"I went up to a couple of art critics, listened to them dissing my work and I agreed with them. I told them that it was derivative and silly and that I was just churning out my greatest hits. Basically, I shot myself in my own foot."

Sutton winced.

"I walked away from them, went into the ladies' room and had a panic attack. Kyle and my mother found me and I begged them for help, begged them to take me to a doctor, but they just shouted at me and left me there, feeling like I was going to die. One of my mother's assistants called an ambulance and I was taken to the hospital. They diagnosed a panic attack, gave me a sedative and I spent the night in the hospital. The next morning they insisted I call a family member so I called Jojo and she came down, picked me up and took me back to Portland."

Sutton stroked the inside of her wrist. "Get it all out, Lowrie."

"Jojo moved me into her house, and I started therapy. Lily and Kyle wanted me to return to Manhattan, but I refused and Jojo told them to leave me alone. Kyle told me I was being childish and irrational and called off our engagement. My mother told me I was spoiled and selfish and was behaving like a brat. I was numb for a couple of months, and because nobody told me to paint, I didn't. And when I finally felt the urge to, I picked up a paintbrush and the anxiety hit me again. I couldn't breathe, my heart felt like it was about to burst out of my chest, so I walked away. Jojo suggested that I go traveling, that I be a kid for a while and I did. I was in Thailand and I emailed Kyle, asking him to transfer funds from my investment account and he refused."

Sutton tensed. "What? Why?"

"He said that I had no funds available, that he'd paid himself and my mother what they were due and used the rest to break the lease on my studio and pay off my debts. I wasn't aware I had any debts."

Sutton lowered his mug, his expression reflecting his shock. "You've got to be kidding me!"

She wished she was. "They took their cuts before I saw any money and I thought I had a million invested, but there was nothing. I sued them and it's still working its way through the court system, with delays and arguments and with the lawyers just getting richer."

Sutton lowered his cup to place it on the table. "I have no idea what to say," he said, shaking his head. "Except that I'm sorry you went through that. That you're still going through that."

"I don't care about the money, to be honest. I've been thinking about calling a halt to the legal proceedings for a while now."

"Why haven't you? Your legal fees must be killing you."

"I can't afford lawyers and I'm not paying the legal bills, Jojo is. She's very wealthy in her own right and refuses to let it drop. She is still furious at my mother for not getting me help, for not seeing that I was burned out, for pushing me so hard. She says it's unconscionable that they took every cent I earned."

"It is," Sutton insisted. "It's your creativity, your talent, and they already took their percentage. It's theft, Lowrie."

Lowrie shrugged. "I gave him power of attorney. I gave him the right to access my funds."

"That doesn't make his actions acceptable and the fact that your mother was party to it astounds me."

"Yeah, well, Jojo is quite sure Lily was swapped at birth," Lowrie quipped. She waved her hand in the air. "Well, that's my why-I-don't-paint-anymore story."

Sutton leaned back in his chair and folded his arms, frowning. "Did you love it?"

She shook her head. "No, I didn't. I adored it. I lived for it. It was my way of making sense of the world."

He didn't speak for a minute, maybe more. "No, you couldn't have loved it that much," he told her, his tone nonconfrontational.

"Before Rhan came along, art was all I cared about!"

"Then why did you give it up? Why, when the panic attacks eased, did you never pick up a palette, a brush, prep a canvas? Was it because you still had their voices in your head, because you still believed that you are second-rate, that you didn't deserve the fame and success you did? You're still marching to the beat of their drum."

"I am not!" Lowrie protested. How dare he say such a thing?

"Yes, you are, or else you would never have let them take away something so important to you."

"I didn't have the money to buy paints or supplies," Lowrie protested, feeling hot and cold.

Sutton's amiable expression didn't change. "Are you seriously telling me that at no point in the past six years you could spare some cash to buy paints, a canvas, a brush? Watercolors? Colored pencils? Charcoal?"

Lowrie glared at him and slouched in her chair, her temper bubbling. "I—I—" Dammit, he was right. And even if she didn't have cash, Jojo would've bought her everything she needed had she said the word. In fact, she did. She recalled Jojo buying canvases, paint and brushes years back and Lowrie had refused to use them. Were they still in the storeroom, where she'd stashed them five years ago? Probably.

"I'm not saying you should produce art to sell, to become the superstar you obviously once were, but don't let them take away your passion, Lowrie."

"I don't know how to paint for fun, Sutton, I never really have." She shrugged. "Maybe when I was a kid. But from my early teens, it was a serious business."

He leaned across the table and literally got in her face. "Then make it unserious, do it for fun, because it makes you feel good. You might not get your money back from them but you can reclaim something you love, something that's yours!"

His words pierced through her defenses, made her take another look at her anti-art stance. She did miss it, but she was scared she'd lost her talent, lost her ability to create. What if she tried to paint something and it was utterly terrible? What then? "I won't be as good as I was before," Lowrie admitted, her voice soft.

She expected Sutton to tell her that she'd be fine, that her talent was just lying dormant, but he didn't. "Of course, you won't be good—you haven't done anything for six years! Whatever you paint or draw will probably be dreadful."

"Well, thank you for that," Lowrie muttered.

"But that's not the point, Low. The point is losing yourself, the point is loving it, the point is finding yourself in the strokes, not how good you are. It's about reclaiming a part of yourself you've denied because your ex-fiancé and mother are awful people." He flashed his megawatt smile. "And have you heard about a concept called practice? I guarantee you'll get better the more you paint."

"And if I get a panic attack, what then?"

"Then you'll get a panic attack and you work through it and deal with it. But I'm willing to bet that the less pressure you put on yourself, the less chance you have of having a panic attack."

He was right, dammit. Her panic attacks were a result of stress and anxiety, and if she went back to art looking to have some fun, with an attitude of kindness toward herself, she probably would be fine.

"Excuse me," Sutton told her, shoving his chair back and heading to where the bathrooms were. She stared as he walked away, annoyed and frustrated with him, but grateful, too. Jojo had tried to talk to her about taking up painting again but she'd shut her down, as she had Paddy. All her attention was dedicated to Rhan, she'd told them. She didn't have time to paint. But she'd left Rhan for nearly a day—something she hadn't done often—and this Manhattan jaunt had shown her that she could leave him for a morning, an afternoon, a couple of hours. She could step away to do things that made her heart sing.

And, God, art did make her heart sing. And dance and twirl.

Maybe, just maybe, she could try again. She wouldn't tell anyone. If she failed, she wouldn't have to give embarrassing explanations. But Sutton was right, she owed it to herself to try.

Because only *she* could reclaim what she'd lost.

Eight

They got back to Portland around two that afternoon and, after parking his luxury SUV in the four-car garage, Lowrie climbed out and immediately dashed down the road to pick up Rhan from Jojo and Isabel.

Smiling at her half walk, half run, Sutton gathered up their bags and took them inside.

He walked into the library and sat on the edge of his desk, taking in the view of the point and the forest, the sea and the sky. He glared at his blank screen, thinking that he needed to do some work, check his emails, call Thea.

Sutton rubbed his hand over his lower jaw, thinking of the last day and a bit, and trying to make sense of it all. He'd thoroughly enjoyed being with Lowrie, much more than he'd expected to. She was one of the few women he knew who didn't rush to fill silences with inane chatter, who was happy to stare out of a window and be with her thoughts. And when they did talk, their conversation was never forced.

He would never have guessed that such a passionate creature existed under that calm facade. She was smoking hot in bed, confident and lusty, and she made his head swim. Sex had been off-the-charts fantastic, the best he'd ever had.

Would he have the honor of sharing her bed again? He didn't know and he couldn't presume. He hoped so, about as much as he wanted to keep breathing. All he could do was ask…

He had known they'd be good in bed—hadn't imagined they'd be fantastic together—but their mental connection *did* surprise him. He'd asked her to tell him about why she didn't paint anymore, but he'd never expected the story he got, was still shocked at how successful she'd been and how her ex and her mother had treated her. He'd been angry—still was— and was astounded by her mother's lack of love, empathy and support,

Jesus, some people were not supposed to procreate. They just weren't good at it, were not able to put their children's needs above their own. Thankfully for Rhan, Lowrie was an excellent parent and he had no doubt Rhan would always come first in her life.

Sutton's adopted mother had been brilliant. In hindsight he could see how involved she'd been in their lives, but what about his birth mother? Had she just been young and dumb? The Tate-Handler Agency only dealt with girls from good families, rich families, so why hadn't she kept him? Was having a baby an embarrassment? What sort of support structure did she have? Was she someone without resources?

There was an envelope in the side pocket of his suitcase—all he needed to do was slit it open, read the letter and find out. But he wasn't ready to do that...not yet.

Maybe not ever.

Sutton stood up and started to pace the L-shaped room, idly looking at the walls covered in old photographs, some of them going back to the early part of the twentieth century.

He remained uninterested in his biological parents, despite meeting members of his birth family last night. Autocratic Callum, easygoing James and Sutton's cousins, Kinga and Tinsley. They seemed nice enough, polite, charming, very glitzy.

But dark waters frequently lurked under placid surfaces.

He'd had a family, a fantastic mother and father, and he'd lost them in an accident. In his teens and twenties, he'd pushed them away, intent to make his own way, laboring under some sort of misguided idea that he wasn't as loved as Thea, that he wasn't really a part of the Marchant family. When they confronted him about his emotional and physical distance, he'd seen the pain on their faces, the sorrow in their eyes.

They weren't at fault—he was, for being so caught up in himself, so damn insecure in his position as their son. But he had been *theirs*, in every way that

was important. After his mental and emotional turn-
about, he'd tried to be the son they wanted, a son to
be proud of, to show them how much he loved them.
But he'd only had two years and he hadn't come close
to making it up to them.

He didn't have the right to another family, and he
wasn't sure he was cut out for one of his own. He
worked too hard, wasn't great at communicating or
showing love and, frankly, could never be half the
dad to his kids his dad had been to him. And if he
couldn't give his children what his dad had given
him and Thea, what was the point? And, yeah, he
really didn't want to have more people in his life he
was scared to lose.

Losing his folks nearly killed him; losing a wife
and child *would*. He wasn't brave enough, he really
wasn't.

So, no. He'd stick to the plan and just do enough to
fulfill the terms of the will, to get his hands on Benjamin Ryder-White's cash. He'd attended the ball, but
he still needed to stay at the inn for another six weeks.

He didn't need to know who his birth mother was,
why she gave him up for adoption or how Benjamin
was connected to this house. It wasn't important…
was it?

But he was curious.

Hell, that couldn't be helped. He was a writer, after
all. But not all questions had to be answered, not all
situations had to be controlled.

"Hey," Lowrie said, walking into the study with

Rhan on her hip. He gripped a hank of her hair and was chortling, happy to be back in his mom's arms.

Sutton couldn't help smiling at the pretty picture they made. "Hi." He nodded at Rhan. "Everything okay?"

"Absolutely fine," Lowrie replied on a wry smile. "I doubt he even noticed I was gone."

Sutton walked over to them and ran a hand over Rhan's head, returning the baby's one-toothed smile. Then Rhan leaned away from Lowrie and toward Sutton, waving his hands in the air. Sutton raised his eyebrows at Lowrie. She shrugged. "He wants you to take him but don't worry, I'll grab a box of toys and put him on the mat."

"I don't mind," Sutton said, placing his hands under Rhan's arms. Rhan laughed as Sutton swung him up and tucked him under his arm like a football.

"It's obvious that you've had some contact with kids," Lowrie said.

"Thea has twin boys, they are seven now. I babysit when she and Sam want to have a date night or a dirty weekend away. We eat junk food and play *Mortal Kombat* or *Assassin's Creed*."

Lowrie didn't hesitate. "I play *Call of Duty* with Rhan—he's pretty good."

Busted. He grinned at her. "Thea would skin me alive. We play *Minecraft* and Xbox soccer."

"Who wins?"

He pulled a face. "They kick my butt, every time. And no, I don't let them win…where's the fun in that?"

Lowrie looked out at the low-hanging clouds and grimaced. "We're in for snow later. Jojo sent me home with a chicken casserole—is that okay for dinner?"

He lifted his free hand and cupped the side of her face. "Are we back to being guest and innkeeper?"

She raised one shoulder and bit her lip. "I don't know... I've never done this before."

She was looking tense again and he knew, by Rhan's suddenly alert body, that he felt it, too. "I loved being with you, Low, and I'd love to be with you again. But that's totally up to you and always will be. Your choice, sweetheart."

"So no offense if I say no?"

His heart clenched at the thought. Damn, being an adult sucked. "No offense. I might pout, but I'll get over it."

She smiled and placed her hand on his waist, resting her forehead on his chest. "Thanks for taking me with you to New York City."

"Thanks for coming with me," Sutton replied, stroking her slim back. He placed a kiss on her temple. Not knowing whether he would be sleeping alone later, he decided to ask. "So, are you saying no, sweetheart?"

She stood up on her tiptoes and brushed her lips across his. "Because Rhan sleeps in his room next to mine, you'd have to temporarily relocate to my bed. Is that okay with you?"

Relief cascaded through him, hot and sweet. And it was strange, because he'd always shrugged off rejection easily before. "Sure," he told her, keeping his voice even while doing cartwheels inside.

Before he could deepen the kiss, as he wanted to, Lowrie stepped back and nodded at Rhan. "Can you entertain him for ten minutes or so while I make coffee?"

"Sure," Sutton replied. He looked at Rhan and made his eyes go squinty, and the baby laughed. "Want to go and watch *Texas Chainsaw Massacre*, kid?"

"He'd prefer something from this decade, Marchant," Lowrie told him, not batting an eye.

Yep, he thought, eying her very nice butt as she walked away, his girl was quick.

Lowrie, glaring at the canvas she'd prepared earlier, was becoming more and more unhinged. It had taken four weeks and a lot of courage for her to dig her paints out of storage and prepare the canvas. She'd arranged for Rhan to spend the day with Jo and Is. Sutton was in the study, pounding his keyboard. She had lots and lots of uninterrupted time to tiptoe back into painting.

Lowrie squinted at her canvas, scowling. Was that a stick insect or a tree? God, the color was horrendous! She'd mixed ultramarine blue and cadmium orange to make brown but it looked too insipid. And, yes, she was out of practice, but her tree looked like a five-year-old had found a tube of beige lipstick and drawn on a wall. The blue under it for the sea was too dark and too thick. It looked flat and, worse, uninteresting and amateurish.

Lowrie placed a hand on her stomach and dropped

to her haunches, staring at the floor. She'd set up her easel in a corner in front of the window. She'd thought she'd start on something familiar, something she'd painted a hundred times before, thinking that muscle memory would take over and she'd fall back into the zone.

But her zone was a car crash.

Had she lost all her talent? Had she forgotten how to paint, to use color? Years ago, she'd mixed paints by instinct, knowing exactly how many squirts of this added to a squirt of that made a particular shade, but judging by the canvas above her, all that knowledge had fled.

She couldn't paint anymore...and the thought was a one-two mental-and-body blow.

Lowrie plopped onto her butt and placed her elbows on her bended knees, her face in her hands. This was a bad, bad, awful idea and she wished she'd never listened to Sutton. Art was part of her past—being Rhan's mom and The Rossi's innkeeper were where she should be focusing her attention. Painting was part of her "before" life. She now lived in the real world and she didn't have time to fool around mixing paints and producing...crap.

Lowrie heard the bedroom door open, but didn't turn around, not wanting Sutton to see her tearstained face. She was angry at herself, angry at him, angry to have gotten her hopes up only to have them so brutally crushed.

"Well, that's pretty bad," Sutton said.

She turned slowly and looked up at him, furious

at the amusement she saw on his face. She leaped to her feet and threw her paintbrush onto the small table she'd set up by the easel. It rolled off the table and splattered brown paint on her floor.

"If you've come up here to mock me then you can just piss off!"

Sutton lifted his hands. "Not mocking you, just stating a fact. It's awful."

"I know!" Lowrie yelled at him. "I've got eyes, don't I?"

Sutton ignored her outburst. "And when I say it's awful, I mean it's awful for you. If anyone else painted it, it would be a perfectly good painting."

"That's not making me feel any better!" Lowrie snapped.

He tucked his hands into the back pockets of his jeans and rocked on his heels. "So what has you so riled up? The fact that you didn't produce an award-winning painting six years after last picking up a paintbrush?"

Yeah, well…exactly! "I didn't expect to be able to paint something good, I just didn't expect it would be so bad. I can't remember how to mix colors the way I used to, my grip on my brush is tight, my perspective is off."

"Yeah, yeah…you're crap," Sutton told her, grinning.

Lowrie punched his biceps. "You are not helping! Go away!"

Sutton wrapped his arms around her waist and rested his chin on her hair. "You're being too hard on yourself, sweetheart. And instead of jumping back into oils, and your type of painting, which requires subtle combinations of color, why don't you ease into it?"

Lowrie scowled. "What, should I get one of those paint-by-number kits?"

Sutton dug the tips of his fingers into her lower back, pushing into tense muscles. "How can you create when you are so damn tense, Low?"

Lowrie released a moan and arched her back, enjoying the way his thumbs pushed into the muscles above her butt.

"And I bet you keep stopping to see if your breathing is shallow, if you feel a little panic."

Yeah, she had being doing that. She had been constantly checking in with her body, testing her lungs, waiting for desperation and stress to flood her system.

"You're being too tough on yourself, Low," Sutton told her, tugging her over to the bed. "You need to trust yourself, and, man, you need to relax. Nobody is judging your work except you."

"You said it was awful," Lowrie pointed out, sighing when his hands slid up under her sweater to dance his fingers over her stomach.

"What do I know?"

"I've always been my own harshest critic," she admitted as he sat down on the edge of the bed and pulled her into the space between his knees.

"And you're judging your work to the standard it was when you were painting constantly and were in high demand, when you were the art world's darling."

Sutton lifted her shirt and dropped an openmouthed kiss on her stomach, just above her belly button. "You can't expect to paint to the same standard, six years after not painting at all."

"I'm not. I just don't want it to look like a dog's breakfast," Lowrie muttered.

"It's a perfectly good attempt for your first time. The second time will be better, the third a lot better… It's like sex. The more we practice, the better we'll get."

Lowrie ran a hand over his burnished head, sighing as his hand slid between the fabric of her panties and the skin of her butt. "You're supposed to be writing, Marchant."

"And you're supposed to be painting. Let's do something else instead."

Oh, yes, please. "*Scrabble*? *Monopoly*? Poker?" she asked, teasing him.

"I'm excellent at *Scrabble*, hate *Monopoly* and I can hold my own in poker. I'll happily show you, later." Sutton looked up and sent her a tender smile. "Take a break, Lowrie, and let me love you."

Lowrie nodded, pushing her fingers in his hair and lowering her head to kiss his mouth. Sutton's hand gripped the back of her head, holding it in place. She slung her leg over his knees and slid down his lap, her doubts, her temper and her frustration melting away. There was only Sutton and what he was doing to her, how he made her feel.

Sutton's hand came up to undo the buttons of her shirt and it fell open, revealing the cups of her lacy, almost transparent baby blue bra. She looked down to see his tanned, broad hand against her pale skin and blue fabric, and sighed. God, she loved the way he touched her, making her feel powerful and feminine and lovely. His hand disappeared beneath the cup of her bra to cover her breast. Her nipple poked his hand and he rubbed her, slowly and gently, building her anticipation.

Lifting her up and off him, he stood and quickly stripped her of her clothes, shoes, socks and yoga pants, dropping her shirt to the floor so that she stood in her matching underwear. He sat back down on the edge of her bed and removed his hiking boots and his socks. She loved his feet—like his hands they were broad, with long toes and neatly clipped nails. Impatient, Lowrie tugged his Henley up his broad chest and over his head, pulling it down his arms. She stroked her hand through the light smattering of hair on his chest, tracing the path that disappeared into his pants. She flat-out adored his body, the strength he exuded.

Looking past his shoulder, she saw that it had started to snow. Big, fluffy flakes drifted past her window to fall on the Juliet balcony outside her room. God, she wanted to capture that blue-white haze, the gray of the sea, the gunmetal-blue of the clouds.

She wanted to paint again—no, she *needed* to paint.

Right damn now.

Lowrie spun back to the table that held her paints and reached for the Payne's gray and pushed a blob onto her palette tray. She grabbed viridian and indanthrone blue, and rapidly mixed them, adding a touch of Portland gray. Yeah, getting there...

Picking up a palette knife, she spread a thick strip across the lower half of the canvas, angling it up to suggest the curve of a wave. Yeah, that was the color—she'd tip it with more gray.

The wave wasn't at the right angle so she smeared her finger through the paint, liking the flow. Sutton came up behind her and placed his hands on her breasts and she stilled, turning to look at him over her shoulder.

"No, don't mind me, carry on," he said. "I'll do the same."

She was excited, her mind hopping between the sensation of his fingers tweaking her nipples and being bombarded by color. Her hand trembled as she mixed paint again, great big blobs of blue and gray and green. She glanced out the window and grabbed a brush, dashing strokes on the canvas, moaning as Sutton's hands dipped down beneath her panties, his fingers working to devastate her control and concentration.

She squinted at the canvas and dragged her brush through some paint, panting as she felt his hard erection pushing into her back, his fingers in her panties, another finger rubbing her nipple—where was her bra and why did she not notice him taking it off?—and soon she couldn't help her harsh breathing as she climbed up and up. Paint splattered on her chest as her hand shook, but she needed to capture the exact roll of that wave about to hit the rock. How should she create that turbulence, capture the power?

In a way, she was trying to paint her orgasm, the buildup to the crash, the intense power locked inside her.

"Open your legs, Lowrie," Sutton said and she did as she was told. Sutton stepped between her and the painting, and dropped to his knees in front of her, his eyes that intense shade of blue she so adored. "Keep painting," he told her, his breath hot on her mound.

"I can't," Lowrie moaned.

"Do it or else I'll stop."

His mouth, hot, wild and experienced, dropped back onto her sex and she bucked against him, her cries the only sound in the room. Lowrie cursed him but she reached for Portland gray and squeezed the paint directly onto the canvas, before adding the dark blue, then green, to the mix. She picked up her palette knife, mixed it and screamed when Sutton's mouth landed on her clitoris. She stopped, dropped her hand to his head and he immediately pulled back. "Paint!"

She looked down at his head, shook hers and dragged her eyes back up to the canvas. She dragged her thumb through the paint, used her palette knife again, and waves started to appear on the canvas, rumbling and grumbling, looking to crash.

God, could she stand it? But Lowrie obeyed his instruction. Immediately her other senses were heightened: she could hear the faint tick-tock of the grandfather clock in the hallway, feel the thud of every heartbeat, smell the acrid turpentine in the bottle on the table. Sutton built her up and up, using his clever mouth and fingers buried deep inside her, as she added white to the tips of the wave…moaning as he stoked her pleasure.

She was going to come…

She slapped her hand against the painting, slid her palm through the paint, then gripped Sutton's bare shoulders, streaking his skin with viridian green and Portland gray. She tipped up her head and lifted her hands to her breasts, playing with her nipples to increase the sensation. She was building, building, about to crash…

Her wave smacked into those rocks, splintering into shards of intense pleasure. Lowrie screamed and shook, and before she was done, Sutton surged to his feet. He scooped her up and tossed her on the bed. Spreading her knees, he slid into her with one smooth stroke, burying himself inside her, and she felt her storm whip up again, another set of waves rushing for shore.

He pulled out and she took him in her fist, guiding him back so that his tip was at her entrance. His biceps bulged with the effort of keeping from ramming himself inside her.

"No condom," he muttered, his arms shaking. He reached across the bed, yanked open a drawer and pulled out a box of condoms. She heard the thud of the box hitting the floor and moaned when Sutton pulled back to sit on his haunches and roll the condom down his length.

"It's so much nicer without a condom," she told him. "Hotter, sexier…"

"Riskier," Sutton muttered, lowering himself down and sliding into her hot, warm channel. "God, you feel so good."

She dug her nails into his butt, laid her mouth on his shoulder and licked his hot, warm skin. She tasted something strange on her tongue and realized it was paint. She laughed and pushed her hands into his hair. They'd be wiping each other down later and wearing turpentine as a perfume, but it was a small price to pay to experience fantastic, mind-blowing, midmorning sex.

"Love me, Sutt," she murmured in his ear.

"I do," Sutton replied as he surged into her, setting off a tsunami deep inside her.

Nine

"I'm going to frame that painting," Sutton said, leaning back against her headboard. "I think it's the best work you've ever done, or ever will do again."

Lowrie looked across to the easel and laughed. Standing up, she walked, naked, over to the painting, picked up a brush and pulled it through the paint mixture on the palette. Writing quickly, she stood back and gestured to her signature in the corner.

"I even signed it for you."

Sutton laughed and patted the bed. He watched Lowrie as she walked back to him, sliding under the covers to nestle into his side. He saw there was paint on her bedspread, across her neck, on her chest. He had no doubt he was dotted with color, too. He couldn't care less.

What he was worried about was whether Lowrie took his words, uttered in the heat of the moment, seriously.

Love me, Sutt.

I do.

And he had, at that moment, never loved anyone or anybody more. But it had been said in the heat of passion and now that reality had returned, those words didn't translate in real life. He liked Lowrie, a lot, but he didn't love her, wouldn't *let* himself love her. He wasn't looking for a lover, or a relationship and, even if he was, she came with a kid, which would mean stepping into an instant family.

He wasn't ready for that, for any of it.

This was a fling, a couple of months of fun, nothing serious.

He had no interest in being Rhan's daddy. He didn't want kids, and he especially didn't want to raise a kid who wasn't his own. His adoption, on the surface picture-perfect, had created many emotional issues, ones he was still working his way through.

Lowrie was the first woman he'd ever met who'd even raised these thoughts in him. Hypothetically, if he and Lowrie fell in love and—very hypothetically now—if they went on to have a kid, maybe more, would he love Rhan as much as he did his own flesh and blood? He didn't know, he wasn't sure, so he'd never put the kid in that position. He wanted to believe that he could but he wasn't certain, so he'd never take the risk.

It wouldn't be fair to Rhan, or to Lowrie, and it would eat him up inside.

But what if he fell for her, realized he couldn't live without her, and what if she, in a year or two or ten, decided he wasn't what she wanted? Would his heart recover from another rejection? Doubtful. No, it was better to avoid pain, put on the brakes and create some emotional distance.

But hell, he'd never had a more exciting, more responsive lover. Passionate, impulsive, creative...

He was definitely getting that painting framed. When he was old, he'd look back and remember their fiery lovemaking on this icy winter morning.

Lowrie kissed his shoulder. "I know you didn't mean it, by the way."

"Pardon?"

She raised those exceptional eyes to his. "You know what I'm talking about, Sutton. I know that you didn't mean it when you said you love me."

Ah.

"You're right, I didn't mean it." He felt her tense and cursed himself for being so blunt. But he didn't know any other way to be. He turned his head away to look out the window. "Love is hard for me, Lowrie," he added, surprising himself. "I'm not good at relationships."

Lowrie reached for the thin blanket at the end of the bed and wrapped it around her torso like a sarong. She sat cross-legged on the bed facing him, her one bent knee resting on his thigh. "Why? Can you tell me that?"

Could he? He didn't know—he wasn't great at talking, but he could try. "I told you that I'm adopted, right?"

Lowrie nodded, her chin in her hand.

"So, Thea, my sister, is the biological child of my adoptive parents. She came along four years after I was born, during a time my parents were trying to adopt another child. She was a complete surprise, as they were told they'd never have kids."

"I've heard that happens," Lowrie said, nodding. "More often than people realize."

"Anyway, Thea is just awesome and she always has been. She quickly became the center of our world. There's a family joke that Thea has an overdeveloped baby finger from winding us around it. As a kid, she was sweet and happy and outgoing and extroverted.

"I was not. I was shy, introverted, supersensitive, but proud with it. People found it difficult to get to know me."

"Found?"

He winced at repeating his use of the past tense. "Was, am. I don't let people in."

"But your parents were good to you? They loved you?"

"Yes." He nodded and rubbed his hand along his jaw. "They loved me as much I would *let* them love me."

"I'm not sure what that means," Lowrie stated, her brow wrinkling.

How to explain? He placed his hand on her thigh and traced patterns on her skin with his thumb, the connection calming him. "I must've been six, maybe a bit older, and I remember my folks sitting down with me and telling me I was adopted. I can't remember the words they used, but I do, distinctly, remember my mom saying that one day, if I wanted to, they'd help me find my *real* parents." He looked away from her, irritated at the ball of emotion in his throat. "Isn't it weird how one little word can have such a massive impact?"

"I don't understand, Sutt."

He loved it when she shortened his name, spoke in that low, sexy, caring tone. "She said she'd help me find my real parents. I've always been sensitive to words and by using the word *real*, to me at age six, that meant they were pretending. That they weren't mine or were only mine until I found my *other* parents. That I didn't have the same relationship with them as Thea did, that I was different."

"I'm sure they didn't mean it like that, Sutton," Lowrie told him. "I'm sure it was just a slip of the tongue."

"It was, I know it was, but it formed the basis of how I saw them for the next twenty-odd years." He lifted his knees but kept his hand on her thigh. "It wasn't something I thought about all the time but it was there. The next time my adoption slapped me in the face was when Thea ran into the house, crying because she'd been told I wasn't her brother. Mom explained about me being adopted, but Thea was so angry and I thought she was mad at me."

"Why?"

"Because in my head, she had a right to have her parents to herself."

"And you're thinking this at what, ten or eleven?" Lowrie asked, puzzled.

"Yeah, I was always an overthinker."

"And far too smart for your own good," Lowrie told him. "What other overly imaginative conclusions did you come to?"

He couldn't object to her phrasing because her words were spot on.

"Because I had this idea they didn't consider me to be a *real* son, I looked for reasons to back up that theory. Did my mom taking Thea shopping mean that she loved her more? If my dad canceled an outing with me, did that mean he didn't want to be with me? I couldn't be honest with them, or vulnerable, because I thought they were looking for an excuse to kick me out. I never disobeyed them, threw a temper tantrum, lost my shit, because I didn't want to lose them."

"Hell, Sutt, it doesn't work like that."

Of course it didn't, but the mind was a powerful weapon when it worked against you. "When I was eighteen, the adoption agency contacted me and my folks and I went to meet with them. They had a letter for me, from my birth mom, but I refused to look at it, to find out who she was or where I came from. My folks pushed me to find out, and, thanks to those childhood fears, I thought they were trying to get rid of me, trying to move me on. I was scared and confused and I took it out on them."

"What did you do?"

"Pulled back, pulled away, tried to put as much distance between myself and them as I could."

"That must've hurt."

"It did, them and me. But in my mind, I'd imposed on them long enough."

God, it hurt to say this out loud, to show her what an idiot he'd been. But she needed to know why he wasn't long-term material, why he could never be in a functional relationship. He bottled everything up, found communicating difficult and created problems for himself and the people who loved him.

"Did your relationship with your parents improve?" Lowrie quietly asked.

He nodded and smiled a little. "But only when I was a lot older. It was shortly before Christmas and I was trying to get out of some family function, I can't remember what. Anyway, my dad drove down from Marchant House, stormed into my office and tore sixty strips off me. He rarely lost his temper, so I just stood there, dumbfounded. He let rip. He told me he was done, that I was hurting my mom with my lack of interest and told me that I had to pull my head out of my ass and act like their son, to be the man they raised me to be. While he stood there, shouting at me, I felt relieved, you know. He wouldn't be this upset if he didn't love me."

Lowrie smiled, understanding.

"Things changed after that and I had two years with them, enjoying every minute of being their son. One Sunday, I was driving them to a local restaurant for lunch and we were in a car accident, a delivery truck T-boned my car. They were killed instantly, and I walked away without a scratch."

She winced, her eyes flooding with tears. "Oh, Sutton, I'm so sorry."

He was, too. "I miss them every day—it's like a hole that won't heal."

"You don't blame yourself for their deaths, do you?"

"No, but I do for distancing myself, for wasting time, for being a self-involved jerk for most of my life. If I'd just told them how I felt, that I felt like a cuckoo in the nest, that I was scared, I wouldn't have so many regrets about how I treated them."

Lowrie stared at him, wrinkling her nose, obviously deep in thought. "I know you probably don't want to hear this, Sutt, but maybe they were at fault, too. Why didn't they push harder to find out why you were distancing yourself? Why didn't they sit you down and demand to know what the problem was? Why did they let nearly ten years pass before your dad lost it? If there's blame to be cast, which I'm not trying to do, then it should be equally shared."

Her words made him feel a little better, a little lighter. "Being English, and upper class, they believed in sporting stiff upper lips, not airing their dirty emotional laundry. As a result, heart-to-heart conversations weren't their thing."

Lowrie smiled. "I can see where you got that from." She turned, lying down on her stomach, and played with the tassels of the blanket. "So have you categorically decided against finding out more about your birth parents?"

"They were just egg and sperm—my family is who raised me. I'm their real child. It took me far too long to realize that."

"Finding out about your birth parents doesn't change that. You can still be your parents' son and explore the circumstances of your birth."

He looked away from her lovely face and debated how to answer her question, considering whether to tell her about Benjamin Ryder-White and his inheritance. When she put it like that, she sounded so damn reasonable and, yeah, he'd be lying if he said he wasn't curious. But he couldn't tell her the whole story yet. He wanted to know why his birth father had sent him to this inn before he discussed Benjamin with her or anyone else.

But he wasn't ready, not yet.

"Why are you really in Portland, Sutton? Why this inn?"

The blaring ringtone coming from his jeans pocket had him leaping out of bed, and he was deeply grateful for the interruption. Saved by the proverbial bell…

"Please ignore it, Sutton, and answer my question," Lowrie insisted, sitting up again. He couldn't, not yet. He'd told her so much already—he couldn't tell her the whole story. Not because he didn't trust her, but because he *did*. He was starting to value her opinion a little too much, seeking her counsel too often. He wasn't a sharing-caring guy. He worked out his own issues by himself. It was the only way he knew how to be.

He shook his head, saw it was a number he didn't recognize and punched the green button. "Marchant."

He watched Lowrie leave the bed, her expression a combination of irritation and resignation. She picked up her clothes and walked into her en suite bathroom, closing the door behind her.

He grimaced and turned his attention back to his call. "Sutton, this is Kinga Ryder-White."

Kinga? Ryder-White? What did she want with him? "Hi there," Sutton said, keeping his voice neutral.

"I'm so glad I caught you! I hear you are still in Portland. Would you like to join me, my siblings and their partners for dinner on Saturday night? And please, feel free to bring a date."

Uh…what?

Looking down at her paint-splattered hands, Lowrie twisted her lips as the hot water of the shower pounded her shoulders. Despite knowing she needed turpentine to remove the paint, she rubbed the bar of soap between her hands, hoping for a miracle.

Sutton had ducked answering her question about why he was in Portland, specifically at this inn. What was he hiding? And why could he tell her deeply personal stuff from his childhood, yet not tell her about why he was in the States?

He'd been far too quick to pounce on that phone, and oh-so happy for an excuse not to answer her question.

You are getting in too deep, Lowrie, allowing your-self to fall.

Sutton was not whom she was looking for, wasn't an answer to her prayers. In fact, he was the last guy in the world she should fall for because he could never give her what she needed.

He buried all his emotions, didn't communicate and wasn't interested in being a dad to her son or to any other children. He was gorgeous and a wonderful lover but he'd rip her heart in two if she was fool enough to give it to him.

So she wouldn't.

Besides, she knew how fickle love could be. Kyle, her manager-fiancé, had misappropriated her money, her mother had abetted him—both were supposed to have loved her. Rex left her when times got tough. No, the only person she could rely on was herself, so she'd stay on her emotional island, her and Rhan, enjoying visits from her grandmother, Isabel and Paddy. Allowing anyone else to take up residence on the safe little patch of earth she'd carved out for herself would be stupid in the extreme.

Sutton was a fling, someone whose body she could enjoy for a few more weeks, and then she'd kiss his cheek and let him go. They were both scarred and scared, and she was old enough to know that two battered, half-alive hearts couldn't make a whole.

Sutton rapped on the door and, not waiting for her reply, stepped inside. She eyed him through the steam, looking at him standing there, his jeans pulled up but not buttoned, his hair messy.

"That was Kinga Ryder-White."

Lowrie looked at him, intrigued. "I wasn't aware that you two knew each other."

"We don't," Sutton said. "We met briefly at the Valentine's Day Ball but that's all the contact we've had. She invited me to join her and her siblings for dinner on Saturday night."

"She only has one sibling—Tinsley," Lowrie said, correcting him.

"That's what I thought but she definitely used the plural."

He'd obviously misheard. If Portland had a prince, they all would've heard about it by now. "So are you going to go?"

He stared down at his bare feet, a million miles away. "Yeah, I think so." Right, so it would be her and Rhan in this huge house on Saturday night. Good to know.

What is wrong with you, Lewis? You've spent plenty of time in this house alone—in fact, you love it! Be honest. It wasn't that she minded being alone—she minded that Sutton was going out to dinner without her.

Grrr…she was acting like she had a claim on his time and attention, and she didn't. They were having a fling, so he owed her no explanations.

"Will you come with me?"

She blinked, unsure of what he'd asked. "Sorry?"

"She said I should bring a date. Will you come?" Sutton asked her, scratching at the streak of paint on his shoulder. "Will Jojo and Isabel take Rhan for the night?"

"I'm sure they will but…are you sure you want to take me?"

He frowned. "Why wouldn't I?"

She shrugged. "Because I'm a single mom innkeeper and they are Portland royalty."

He frowned at her. "Yes, and you are also an incredibly talented artist and an interesting woman, Lowrie. Stop putting yourself down."

Right. Okay, then. She wanted to argue with him but he was right. There was nothing attractive about self-bashing. "Is the dinner at a fancy restaurant?"

"I'm not sure. She said she'd text me the directions. So is that a yes?"

She nodded. "Yes, please. And thank you."

Sutton grinned and gestured to her torso. "You have gray paint on the side of your left breast. And on your stomach."

She lifted up her hands for him to see. "And you have it on your shoulder and down your back," she told him. "Can you grab the turpentine and the rag? I'll get yours off if you remove mine."

His smile turned wolfish. "I like the way you think, Lewis."

"I'm talking about paint, Marchant," Lowrie told him, keeping her voice prim.

"I'm not," Sutton replied, turning away to get the turpentine and the rag. She sighed and hoped he remembered to grab a condom. After such a physical morning, she might just need a nap.

* * *

Kinga Ryder-White opened the door to her apartment and welcomed them. Sutton took Lowrie's coat, introduced her to Kinga and followed Kinga into her apartment, his eyes bouncing from person to person in the room. Tinsley stood by the fireplace, a glass of red wine in her hand. She was laughing at something Jules Carson was telling her. Garrett Kaye, the venture capitalist, sat on the arm of Jules's chair, his hand lightly cupping the back of her neck. Sutton had thought they'd been sparking off each other at the Valentine's Day Ball and they were now, obviously, together. Good to know he wasn't wholly unobservant.

Sutton shook hands with Garrett, Kinga's fiancé, Griff O'Hare—the announcement was headline news for a couple of days—and Cody Gallant, who stood with his arms around Tinsley's waist. Right, everyone was loved up...

Good for them.

He looked across at Lowrie, who'd been tugged down to sit between Jules and Kinga and had accepted an offer of wine from Griff.

"Sorry about the lack of space," Griff told him, when he had a drink in his hand. "Kinga and I are looking for a bigger place but we haven't found anything yet."

"Are you going to build?" Cody asked him.

"Maybe," Griff replied. "But I'm doing a minitour in a few months and we'd have to meet with an architect and come up with plans before that happens. And then Kinga would have to supervise the build and she's got more than enough on her plate right now."

Garrett wandered over to join them, his face relaxed and happy. "Nice to see you again, Sutton. How goes the writing?"

Sutton winced. His word count lately was dismal. But because he hated to whine, he just shrugged. "It goes." He looked over to Jules, who was laughing at something Lowrie said. Wanting to get the spotlight off him, Sutton recalled a long conversation at the ball about a gin-making company out west.

"What happened with Crazy Kate's? I remember us discussing its downward spiral at the ball. Was it liquidated?"

Garrett smiled. "We managed to pull a rabbit out of the bag and Crazy Kate's was saved. They are back in production with Kate, Jules's second mother, at the helm. Kate also has a new financial adviser who keeps her on the straight and narrow."

He said the words with such fondness that Sutton had no problem working out the subtext. "You?"

Garrett nodded. "Me. In between being the co-CEO of Ryder International and Crazy Kate's adviser and trying to keep up with Jules, I'm exhausted."

He might be tired, but the guy looked happy. Good for him. Hold on…

"Wait…what did you say? You are involved in Ryder International now? How did that happen?"

Garrett sipped his whiskey. "Well, you know Callum had a heart attack, right?"

He'd heard that along the way. "Yeah, but he's okay, right?"

"He's still in the hospital, slowly recovering after picking up an infection. Anyway—"

"Food is ready!" Kinga called from the kitchen area of the open-plan space.

"Hold that thought," Garrett told Sutton as Lowrie asked Kinga whether she'd cooked.

Kinga tossed her bright blond head and laughed. "No, I don't like to poison my dinner guests. Griff and I love a little Italian place down in Old Town called Benito's—"

"I know it, my uncle used to take me there as a little girl," Lowrie told her.

Kinga flashed her a smile. "My dad used to take us, too. He told me *his* uncle introduced him to Benito. I know it's been around for more than seventy years. Anyway, it's their lasagna. And garlic bread. But I made the salad."

"Avoid the salad, people," Griff teased her, walking past and stopping to drop a kiss on her temple.

Kinga tried, unsuccessfully, to swat him with a kitchen towel.

Ten minutes later they all sat around the too-small dining table, bumping elbows and jostling for food, finding space on the crowded table for wine bottles and glasses. Lowrie sat opposite him, in between Griff and Garrett, a huge smile on her face.

He caught her eye and mouthed, *You okay?*

She nodded and slid her eyes to the left, to where Griff was sitting next to her, and placed her hand on her heart, closing her eyes. He rolled his eyes. "Funny girl," he said, remembering their conversation about Griff's hotness.

"Isabel is going to hate me forever," Lowrie told him, grinning. Seeing that the rest of the table were now listening to their exchange, he sat back and grinned at Lowrie, lifting his eyebrow in a challenge to explain.

She didn't hesitate, just turned to Griff and shrugged. "You ring my aunt's bell. She's never going to forgive me for being thigh-to-thigh with you."

Both Kinga and Griff laughed, as did the rest of the table. Griff turned to Kinga and winked at her. "Competition, babe."

"Yeah, yeah…" Kinga rolled her eyes. "Trust me, I will not miss your inability to pick up your clothes or replace the toilet roll."

"We've been engaged like ten minutes and she's already nagging me," Griff complained good-naturedly. He turned to Lowrie. "What do you do, Lowrie?"

"I run an inn, situated on the water in East End." She looked at Sutton and he frowned, silently telling her to own her art. "A long time ago I was an artist, a painter. I was pretty successful."

Sutton winked at her, there was admiration in his eyes, and she shrugged, embarrassed.

"Do you not paint anymore?" Jules asked, interested.

He wondered how she was going to answer. "Ah, I was young and I didn't know how to handle the pressure, the success and the attention. I had a bit of a meltdown and I went traveling for a long time. And then I got pregnant so my uncle's ex offered me a job at the inn they converted on the bay."

"You have a baby?" Jules asked, clapping her hands.

"Yes, a boy. He's a little over a year. His name is Rhan."

"I'd love to see a picture," Tinsley said, and Lowrie picked up her phone, scrolled through the gallery and then passed it around. He caught a picture of Rhan, toothy smile and dark eyes, and his heart turned over. He was such a gorgeous kid, happy and chill.

"Have you seen Callum lately, Cody?" Garrett asked, tearing off a piece of garlic bread from the loaf in front of him.

Sutton's attention moved away from the conversation about Rhan and he waited for Cody's answer.

"He's still frail but getting terser with every interaction. I presume that means he's getting better," Cody replied. "When I saw him yesterday, he went on a ten-minute rant about James and his inability to track down the owner of Benjamin's shares. Then he spent another ten minutes bitching about the fact that he can't get his DNA results back from that genealogy company."

"What is the holdup?" Kinga asked, tuning back into the conversation. "We swabbed our mouths on Christmas Eve, it's now the third week of March and we've heard nothing. Other people have gotten their results within a week or two of submitting their samples."

Tinsley saw his and Lowrie's confusion and laid a hand on his arm. "Sorry, quick explanation. Our grandfather is obsessed with his DNA and the fact that he is the last of an unbroken line of Ryder-Whites—"

"Well, technically, Dad is," Kinga corrected her.

"Yeah, but Callum doesn't like Dad, so he considers himself the reigning king… Anyway, he gave us the present of having our genealogy traced by a local company and we can't get the results back."

Sutton frowned. "That's strange. My sister had it done in the UK and it was quick."

Kinga shrugged. "I know, that is what we're having difficulty with."

Sutton picked up his wineglass, sipped and decided to return to his earlier conversation with Garrett. "Garrett, you were going to tell me how you came to be involved with Ryder International?"

Garrett pushed a hand through his hair. "It's not public knowledge yet…" He trailed off. He looked at Kinga, then Tinsley.

Kinga nodded and spoke. "You can tell Sutton, Garrett. I don't think he or Lowrie are going to run to the tabloids. And if they do, so what?"

Garrett shared his smile between the sisters, his expression a little tender. Not an emotion Sutton expected to see on the hard-as-nails venture capitalist's face.

"My mother is Callum's personal assistant and from the time I was a teen, I thought Callum was my father. It turns out that James is my dad," Garrett explained.

Sutton raised his eyebrows in astonishment. "Really?"

"Yeah. When Callum had his heart attack, he told James to find someone to run Ryder International. He and James have a fraught relationship and there isn't a great deal of affection between them—"

"Or any at all," Kinga interjected.

"Despite knowing that it might jeopardize his inheritance, James decided to reveal that I was his son. James also offered me the Ryder CEO job and left it up to me whether or not to acknowledge him as my father. I have, privately, and he, Kinga, Tinsley and I are running Ryder International together."

Well, that was bombshell news.

"Will Callum go back to work at Ryder International?" Lowrie asked.

Garrett shrugged. "I'm sure he will, at some point. Hopefully by then we will have locked in some permanent changes, changed some of his old-fashioned policies."

"Like?" Sutton asked, obviously interested. He owned a significant share of the company in question. Or shortly would.

"We want to restructure the company and streamline it. Worldwide, upper and middle management is top-heavy and there's a massive overlap between jobs. We want equal pay for equal work. It's nonsense that men earn fifteen percent more than their women colleagues," Kinga said, sounding crisp. "Paternal leave, better employee benefits. We've encountered some resistance to the changes from the old guard of managers and are expecting more from Callum's cronies on the board of directors."

"James sent a letter to the lawyers representing our silent-but-powerful shareholder, asking him for our support for these changes. If he sides with us, we'll have enough votes at the upcoming board meeting to push them through."

Kinga smiled and looked at Lowrie, seeing her confusion. "Someone out there controls what used to be my uncle Benjamin's shares in Ryder International. We don't know who it is—he hides behind a blind trust."

Sutton started to object to the word *hides* and then remembered that they didn't know he was on the cusp of taking ownership of the shares. And he wasn't about to disclose that at a family dinner, the second time he'd been in the company of the Ryder-Whites. He caught Lowrie's frown and watched her tip her head to the side. He wondered what she was thinking.

Sutton took a large sip of his wine and forced himself to lift a forkful of lasagna to his lips. He chewed, tasting nothing, and when there was a gap in the conversation, he spoke again. "So your uncle Benjamin was Callum's brother?"

Tinsley picked an olive off her plate and popped it into her mouth. "Mmm, he was a great deal younger than Callum, fifteen or twenty years I think."

"And did they get along well?"

"God, no, they hated each other! Well, Callum hated Ben, and really loathed that he wouldn't marry and settle down," Tinsley replied. "Callum never accepted Ben being gay and thought he could switch his sexual preferences at will."

"He was *gay*?" Sutton spluttered. That couldn't be right. He was here after all.

Seven pairs of eyes hit his face, all cool. He immediately lifted his hands, not blaming them for assuming he was intolerant. But he couldn't tell them that he'd just found out that his birth father was gay. Or, he thought, as his brain restarted, at the very least, bisexual at some point in his life.

"Sorry. That came out all wrong…" He cleared his throat, annoyed to feel heat in his cheeks. "I'm not that guy, I promise. I don't give a toss what people do in the privacy of their bedrooms."

"He's really not," Lowrie assured them and he smiled his thanks when six spines relaxed.

"By the way, my uncle Carlo was gay and he and my uncle Paddy established the inn together. They were together for more than thirty years. The LGBTQ community in Portland back then was smaller than it is now. I wonder if they knew each other?"

"What was his surname?" Tinsley asked.

"Rossi," Lowrie said and frowned when Tinsley and Kinga both gasped.

Tinsley's knife falling onto her bone china plate shattered the silence.

"Oh, my God," Kinga said, placing her hand on her heart.

Lowrie hunched her shoulders and looked from them to Sutton, as if asking him what she should do.

He had no idea so he shrugged. "I'm sorry, we don't understand."

"Our uncle, the one we were talking about? Well, he had a lover named Carlo Rossi. They were living together when he died, living in Carlo's house somewhere on the bay," Kinga explained.

"My uncle and your uncle?" Lowrie demanded, her eyes wide.

Kinga clapped her hands together, her eyes sparking with the thrill of the unexpected. "Oh, my God, can you believe it?"

Sutton stared at his plate while the table erupted. Well, now he knew why he'd been sent to spend time at Carlo's inn.

Ten

Because he wasn't the chattiest kid in the sandbox, nobody noticed that Sutton, as the evening progressed, got quieter and quieter and retreated into an all but unreachable space. Oh, he answered when he was spoken to, spoke just enough so nobody realized anything was off, but because she'd been living with him for nearly two months, Lowrie saw the distance in his eyes, the pull of his lips, the tension in his shoulders.

He was upset, but she couldn't fathom why.

Leaning back in her seat as Sutton drove them home, she thought back on the evening. She'd had a lot more fun than expected and would love to hang out with the group a little more. Instead of being the prissy princesses she expected, Kinga and Tinsley were down-to-earth and lovely, strong women, but not without empathy. They were quick to laugh, quick to tease.

Lowrie had been so sure that being alone on her emotional island with Rhan was what she wanted, but now, after seeing the way the extended Ryder-White clan interacted, she wasn't so certain. She could do with a couple of girlfriends, lunches and coffee dates, feminine conversation that rambled and rolled along. She'd been so busy with Rhan, with the inn, but now she felt like she was missing out. She wanted more people in her life who loved her, or at least liked her. She wanted to socialize, to laugh and tease. Have more people her own age in her life.

And, God, the relationship those women had with their men! There was no doubt those couples were all deeply in love, that they'd found their forever partners. Lowrie and Sutton were sleeping together, that much was obvious, but there was a mental distance between them that was easy to discern. They knew each other in bed, but emotionally? They'd barely connected at all.

And Sutton was doing what he always did—he was blocking her out and trying to unravel the mystery on his own. Oh, she knew he was a loner, that his career as a novelist was both lonely and, sometimes, unexplainable, but he didn't have to figure out everything solo. Why wouldn't he let her in? Let her help?

She was crazy about him, Lowrie admitted. Might even be on the way to being neck-deep in love with him. She loved his body, his small smiles, his occasional sense of the ridiculous. She loved his confidence, his I-don't-give-a-crap attitude. He was a strong man but, at his core, he was a loner...

She'd fought for love her whole life, banged on people's doors asking them to love her—not her talent or her success—and she was damned if she'd ever do that again. A life spent with Sutton would be spent prodding and prying, trying to get him to open up, to let her in. And, as she'd been taught, love not freely given wasn't love at all.

They didn't have a future. It was time to accept that—and God, it felt like a thousand hornet stings. But even accepting they weren't a couple, she knew he was her friend. She was utterly unable to sit here and let him stew on his own.

"Want to tell me why you are rattled?" she asked, turning to look at his strong profile.

"I'm fine," he politely answered. "Did you have fun?"

"I did and you know it. And you are trying to change the subject," Lowrie said, too tired to play games. Sutton signaled to turn onto her road and she winced. She'd left this conversation far too late and they were home. In the car he was a captive audience, but now that they were back at the inn, if Sutton didn't want to talk, he could remove himself to more than a dozen rooms in the building and there was nothing she could do about it.

"I need a drink," Sutton told her, pulling into the garage. He exited the vehicle, walked around to her side and opened the car door for her. His action was instinctive, but his expression suggested she should leave him alone.

Well, that wasn't going to happen.

Sutton opened the side door, entered through the utility room and shrugged off his jacket. Without putting on any lights, he walked through to the sea-facing lounge, his back ramrod straight.

Lowrie hung her coat on the coat stand and flipped on the hallway light. She hung up her scarf and handbag on another hook and debated whether to let Sutton stew.

No, when he stomped around too much in his own head, he overanalyzed and overthought, and that wasn't healthy. Besides, she thought she might be in love with him—Damn! Damn! Damn!—and she'd do anything to ease his pain.

Because he was in pain, any fool—or any woman foolish enough to fall in love with the man—could see it.

He stood at the tall windows, his forearm resting on the glass above his head, and stared down at the ink-black rocks. He cracked a window and an icy breeze sent shivers down her spine. Sutton held a whiskey tumbler in his other hand.

Lowrie sat down on the arm of the closest chair and crossed her legs, linking her hands around her knees. "Talk to me, Sutt."

He didn't reply but she did catch the quick shake of his head.

"You told me that had you communicated better when you were a kid and young adult, then you wouldn't have jumped to so many conclusions about your parents, that you wouldn't have wasted so much time."

He spun around, his expression bordering on mean. But she wasn't scared—he would never, ever hurt her.

"That's a low blow."

She shrugged. "It's the truth." And the truth could hurt in a thousand different ways. "Tell me about why you are here in Portland, staying in my house."

He turned his back on her again, his spine rigid with tension. She waited and then waited some more. Five minutes passed, then a few more, and Lowrie finally realized that he didn't trust her enough, respect her enough or care for her enough to let her in. Right, she didn't need him to draw her a picture.

She didn't need to love someone who couldn't love her back, who kept her on the outside looking in. She'd done that all her life—with her mom, with Kyle, with Rex. They'd loved her on their terms, not hers. She'd never again settle for less than everything—a mental and emotional connection and complete trust. Maybe she was shooting for the impossible, but she'd rather be alone than have less than what she wanted.

Lowrie stood up and started walking to the door, her shoulders hunched and her hands in the back pockets of her smart woolen pants. She blinked away the moisture in her eyes, annoyed to find her eyes wet. He wasn't worth her tears.

"Benjamin Ryder-White is my birth father."

His words reached her, his tone low and confused. It took her a good thirty seconds to process what he'd said, and when she did, she softly whistled. Right, well, she hadn't expected that.

Lowrie walked over to where he was standing and

leaned her shoulder into the wall, her eyes on his pro-file. "How long have you known?"

"Mid-January. I turned thirty-five and the adop-tion agency lawyers met with me."

She had a million questions running through her head. "How did the adoption agency know he was your birth father?"

"I can only presume that my birth mother told him and he contacted the agency."

Eh, okay, that made sense. But she still didn't un-derstand why Sutton was here, in Portland. So she asked him. A muscle jumped in Sutton's jaw as he lifted the glass of whiskey to his lips. It was nearly half-gone, she noticed. Sutton wasn't a big drinker so seeing him put back so much liquor at one time was a good indicator as to how upset he was.

"I'm about to inherit a crapload of money from him, as well as his twenty-five-percent share in Ryder International."

"The same shares that were discussed earlier, the ones that Callum Ryder-White is so desperate to get his hands on?"

He nodded.

"God, you're seriously rich."

Her asinine comment almost made him smile. "I was rich before, but yeah, this puts me up a level."

"Are the shares why you are in Portland?"

He rocked his hand up and down. "There were two codicils to me inheriting his wealth. The first is that I had to spend two months here, at this inn. I can only think that Benjamin wanted me to be here, to find out about him and his life through Carlo. Judging by the hatred between Benjamin and his brother, I think he wanted his story to be told by someone who loved him. The other proviso was that I attend the Valentine's Day Ball, I presume because it, and the foundation, was something he started and was proud of."

Lowrie shrugged, thinking it was so sad that Carlo had passed and couldn't tell Sutton about the man he'd loved such a long time ago. She thought for a minute. "Paddy and Carlo were together for thirty years, Sutton—maybe Paddy knew Benjamin? Or knew about him from Carlo?"

"I doubt Carlo would've spent any time talking about his old lover to his new lover," Sutton muttered, dragging his hand through his hair.

"Paddy and Carlo knew each other all their lives, they were friends long before they became lovers. Maybe Paddy even met Ben, knew him."

"But I don't need to know anything about Benjamin, Lowrie!" Sutton turned anguished eyes onto her. "You keep mistaking me for someone who cares. I don't care about anything except fulfilling the terms of the will, getting my hands on that fortune."

"So you're just in it for the millions?"

He shrugged, not bothering to dispute her statement. No, that couldn't be true. Sutton, who wore casual jeans and sweatshirts, wasn't that into money... but God, what did she know? It wasn't something they'd spoken about. And if she was wrong about the money, what else had she misconstrued? What was his real reason for being with her?

"Then what am I? A side benefit?"

He didn't look at her. Lowrie pushed her hands into her hair and tugged at the strands, not sure whether or not to smack him. He was hurting, of that she was sure, but he was also acting like a prime-grade jerk.

But she did sense that this was a watershed conversation, something that would make or break them. He'd either knock down some of his walls and talk to her, or he'd layer another brick on top, making entry into his inner world impossible.

"Come and sit down, Sutton, and talk to me. Let me in, let me talk this through with you. I can see that this has upset you—"

He whirled around, his eyes blazing. "This? You've got to be joking! In the scheme of things, this is barely a scratch. This means *nothing*. Compared to losing my parents, my real parents, this doesn't even blip on my radar! She gave me up, he gave me up... I don't give a shit about them!"

Oh, he cared more than he thought. "Then why are you shouting?"

"I'm shouting because you won't stop bugging me! I'm shouting because you won't leave me the hell alone! And yes, you were a side benefit to being in this cold-as-hell place, a way to pass the time, to relieve the boredom."

She knew he didn't mean that, not really, but his words came too close to others she'd heard before— *you're a meal ticket, you're a fun time*—and they stung like the slash of a steel-edged whip across her soul. Lowrie lifted her head and her eyes, roiling with anger and frustration, clashed with his. And an emotion she couldn't place, something hard and feral.

Maybe he did mean it. Maybe she was simply someone he'd been using.

Because, if she was honest, she was the ultimate fling. She not only washed his clothes and tidied up after him as his housekeeper, but she also warmed his bed at night. He didn't have to make any effort to see her, to make plans with her, since she was always available. Living in the same house, he didn't need to lift a finger...

God, she'd been such an idiot to think he was different! She was simply convenient.

Hurting everywhere, from the tips of her hair to the nails on her toes, she cursed her burning eyes. She walked in the direction of the door and bumped her knee into the side table.

She felt movement behind her, heard him calling her name.

She spun around. "Don't! Don't you dare apologize. It'll mean nothing and my respect for you, already skimming rock bottom, will drop exponentially. Stay in your messed-up mind, Sutton. Be on your own. Keep using people, stay apart, be the loner you so desperately want to be. But know that when you are eighty or a hundred, and sitting in your study surrounded by musty books, you'll regret me. You'll regret not allowing love into your life."

"You haven't let love into your life," Sutton pointed out, his voice raw with emotion.

"Because I fell for another man who couldn't give

me what I need! A repressed Englishman who thinks too much and feels too little," Lowrie snapped. "Your parents loved you, but you were too scared to accept that love. I'm crazy about you, but yet again, you are running away. There's another family out there who'd be happy to let you into their lives—Kinga and Tinsley are lovely people—but because you are so damn scared, you'll take Ben's money and run back to your ivory tower. I only realized this earlier tonight, but do you know what I would do for sisters, friends, for more people in my life to love me, to love Rhan? You can never have too much love in your life, but somehow you're above all that!"

He opened his mouth to speak but shut it again and shook his head. Yeah, talking to him, shouting, was like shouting at a brick wall. "Stubborn, stupid man!" she muttered before spinning on her heel and storming out of the room and into the hallway.

She grabbed her coat, wrapped her scarf around her neck and stepped into the cold night, needing to get to Rhan and Jojo. To Isabel.

To be with the three people who loved her, no questions asked.

Sutton followed her down the road to Jojo's, just to make sure she got there safely. That she didn't, in her anger, slip on some ice, crack her head and lie on the sidewalk for the rest of the night.

From the shadows of the hedge, he saw the front door to her grandmother's house open and watched

Jojo pull her inside and into her arms. He was too far away to see, but he knew that Lowrie was crying.

He'd done that. And so much more.

Walking back to the inn, Sutton scrubbed his hands over his face, as cold on the inside as he was on the outside. What an intense, soul-disturbing evening.

He jammed his hands into the pockets of his coat and stared up at the star-filled sky. He wasn't a praying man, but he could do with some divine guidance because, God, his life was so fucked up.

He was Benjamin's son. He liked his second cousins—a lot—and a part of him wanted to get to know them better. He liked their men and thought he and Garrett could become good friends. Thea would adore them all. They were her type of people—smart, funny, direct…down-to-earth. He had, if he wanted it—if they wanted him—a family…

But it wouldn't fill up the hole that had been carved out when Lowrie stormed away. If he had to choose between her and the Ryder-Whites, between her and anyone else, ever, he'd choose her. But she came with a kid and that little guy—that gorgeous kid—scared him like no other. Sutton wouldn't just be living his life with Lowrie, he'd also become Rhan's stepdad, his role model, his dad but *not* his dad. In his life but not his blood.

Sutton and Lowrie were adults. They could choose whom to love, but their choices would affect Rhan. What if Sutton raised him and then things fell apart with him and Lowrie? How would Rhan feel, what would he do? How would *Sutton* feel?

Or, if Sutton and Lowrie had other kids, would Rhan feel less loved, not as good? And what if Lowrie, in a couple of years, left Sutton? He wouldn't just lose her, but Rhan, too. Sutton jammed his fist into his sternum, trying to push away the sharp pain.

He couldn't think about Lowrie, couldn't deal with her and the complications loving her pulled to the surface. Before he tackled Lowrie and her place in his life—or his in hers—he had to sort out the Ryder-White mess.

He needed to get all the facts, face the truth of his birth and how he came into this life, once and for all. He'd been picking and choosing his puzzle pieces, trying to fit them into a picture where they didn't belong. He needed to put the right pieces in the right places and go from there.

He needed to face the truth, find out who his birth mother was, what caused her to give him up and deal with any emotional fallout.

Until he worked out how to deal with his past— all of his past—he wouldn't be able to construct his future.

The future that had just stormed out of this house and down the road, the future that included the baby boy he was damn sure she was cuddling.

Sutton arrived back at the inn, shed his coat in the hallway and walked up the stairs to his room. He walked over to the freestanding wardrobe, pulled down his suitcase and flung it on the bed. Lifting the lid, he saw the outline of the envelope in the inside pocket, his throat Sahara-dry.

God, he wished Lowrie was here, sitting next to him, her hand on his back as he perused its contents. But because he was a selfish, silent prick with the communication skills of a cactus, she'd bolted. And he only had himself to blame.

Get on with it, Marchant.

He dipped his hand inside the pocket, pulled out the envelope and walked over to the comfortable chair in the corner. He sat down and stared at his trembling fingers. This was it.

He looked across the room to where a photograph stood of his parents, wrapped in each other's arms, laughing at the camera.

It's okay, Sutton, you can do this. And you will always and forever be ours.

Sutton blinked away his tears, grateful to hear his mother's voice in his head, suddenly sure that if she knew of this, she'd be here, supporting him. The woman in the envelope might've birthed him, but those were his parents, the people who'd made him the center of their world.

He loved books because his mom read to him every night, knew how to crack an egg one-handed because he'd watch his dad make breakfast every Sunday morning—eighties rock music blaring—for eighteen or so years. He loved Monty Python, astronomy, watching Wimbledon tennis because his parents did. So much of what was important in his life, his opinions and his values, he'd inherited from that couple who didn't pass on a single strand of DNA to him. And as he later learned, the day she heard about him being adopted, Thea cried because she'd been terrified someone was going to take her big brother away.

He was a Marchant, and always would be. Nothing in the envelope could change that. Nothing ever would. Feeling calmer—heart still aching but calmer—he ripped open the package and pulled out a thin envelope. He looked at the corner, saw the stamps on the expensive stationary and saw that the letter was postmarked the first day of the New Year, the year he was born.

Removing the rubber band, he picked up the letter, his heart pounding. Forcing his finger under the seal, he pulled out the thick, expensive paper.

Dear Sutton…

I hope they've kept the name I chose for you. From the time I was little, I wanted a boy and two girls. I just never expected to have a boy under these circumstances… I know that you are a boy, don't ask me how.

It's winter in London and I turned nineteen a few months ago, a year older than you are now, assuming you're reading this on your eighteenth birthday. I am sitting in the apartment my parents hired for me in Mayfair, and it's a cold, bleak day. I can feel you moving around inside me, and they say you are going to be a big baby. Honestly, I'm a little terrified of how I'm going to push a six-pound baby into the world. But I will, I have no choice. Just like I have little choice but to be in this apartment, on a rainy Monday in January.

I suppose I am the embodiment of a "poor little rich girl." I'm an only child of a timber industrialist and his society wife, both active in conservative politics and the leading lights of East Coast society. Blue bloods, if you will. We're the American equivalent of royalty, or so my parents and their friends like to think. We live by a code, anything—drugs, promiscuity, alcohol, bad business deals—is acceptable provided we don't get caught, that our peccadilloes don't become public knowledge. We must be seen as above reproach, perfect in every way. Hypocritical, I know.

Falling pregnant by a man fifteen years older than me is not acceptable. Neither is an abortion. I have tried to talk to your father, but he's managed to avoid me for the past nine months. You can do that when you are rich and powerful. As a result, I am reliant, in every way possible, on my parents. They have the money, the power and, should I buck their wishes, I will be the poor girl without a place to live or a cent to my name. I wish you and I could just run away, but how would I feed you, us? How could I work and look after you? I want to think that I am brave enough to try, strong enough to struggle, but I'm not. I'm quite spoiled, you know.

So I agreed to come here to London, to engage with an agency who specializes in dealing with little rich girls who get themselves in trouble. My friends back home think I'm at finishing school in Switzerland. It's 1987, for God's sake, who goes to finishing school anymore?

Anyway…adoption it is. I know a little about the people who are going to take you, though not their names, and they seem like good people. They are, I'm told, so excited to take you home, to make you theirs. You'll have a good life with them, of that I am sure.

I wish I was stronger, better, less spoiled, more resilient. But I'm not, and I can't pretend to be. I only hope that your new mother and father raise you to be a better person than I am.

My name is Penelope Freya Jackson and the man who made me pregnant is Benjamin Ryder-White. Should you wish to, when you are an adult, you can track me down. I imagine I'll be easy enough to find.

Penelope Ryder-White, Kinga and Tinsley's mother, was his mother, too.

They weren't his cousins, but his half sisters.

Sutton stood up, intent on telling Lowrie the news, desperate to share this information with her. He looked around, remembered that they weren't talking—might never again—and sank back down onto the bed.

Holy, holy shit.

What the hell was he going to do?

Eleven

Penelope

The last time Penelope had met with her private investigator, it had been in this same coffee shop. And young KJ Holden had ordered an espresso that time, too.

Today, Penelope hoped there was more information to share.

"So thank you for meeting with me today." KJ leaned forward and dropped her voice so that she couldn't be overheard by people at the adjacent tables. "As you know, I tracked down the adoption agency and I asked them for information on your son. I wasn't surprised when they refused to entertain my inquiries. They told me that if he wanted to contact you, he knew how to do that."

Penelope swallowed down her impatience. Of course, she knew this, found it incredibly frustrating. How could she control events if she had no cards to play, and wasn't even sitting at the poker table?

KJ tapped her finger against her coffee cup. "Imagine my surprise when the lawyer representing the agency contacted me and told me that your son is looking for a meeting."

What?

Penelope jerked back her head, feeling like she'd been slapped. Immediately, she glanced toward the door, wondering how long it would take her to stumble into the cold air, to find her car and start driving. And driving. And driving.

"They asked me to facilitate a meeting between you and the son you gave up for adoption."

Penelope was going to meet her son; her secrets would come to light. She didn't know if she could bear it. Her friends, her family, her girls… *James.*

God, she still hadn't told him. How would he react? Would he hate her, yell at her, refuse to talk to her?

No…wait! James told her that they were stronger together. There wasn't anything they couldn't handle. She just had to believe that. She hadn't held his past against him; he would deal with hers. She had to trust him.

As for the girls, well, they were more resilient than she'd ever imagined. But how would Callum react?

Did she even care? She'd never liked her father-in-law and no longer gave a hooey about his feelings!

Penelope met KJ's sympathetic eyes, then straightened her spine and lifted her chin. She was a Jackson by birth and a Ryder-White by marriage and blue bloods didn't buckle.

"Say what you need to and get it done," Penelope told her through gritted teeth.

"Up until this point in his life, he had no intention of meeting you. But circumstances are dictating that he makes his presence known, and this specifically relates to the shares he owns in Ryder International."

She *knew* it, knew that Ben would've made provisions for him, made sure that *his* blood inherited *his* share of Ryder International. The Ryder-White men shared a craving for continuity.

"Who is he?" Penelope asked again, her voice high and tight. "And when am I going to meet him?"

KJ looked toward the door of the diner. "Right now, if that suits you. If it doesn't, then you can meet at some point in the future." She pulled a face. "I have been asked to tell you that, due to circumstances, you will probably run into each other quite frequently so maybe it's best to get this over with."

Get this over with? *This* was only meeting her child, the son she never knew! Penelope fanned her fingers over her heart and took a deep breath, looking for her courage, telling herself she couldn't cry, wouldn't cry.

She would not embarrass herself like that. *Stiff upper lip, dammit!*

"Who is he?" she whispered.

"His name is Sutton Marchant and, when you are ready—*if* you are ready—he's waiting outside," KJ softly told her. "I just need to call him and he'll either come in or go away."

Penelope closed her eyes and bit the inside of her lip, so hard that she drew blood. She opened her eyes, leaned back in her chair and finally nodded. "Call him. Do it now before I change my mind."

Sutton stood outside Callum Ryder-White's study at his home in Yarmouth and leaned his shoulder into the wall, waiting—as were James, Kinga, Tinsley and Garrett—for Callum to admit them into his inner sanctum.

The old codger was taking his time.

Sutton ran a weary hand over his face and wanted this day done, this part of his life over. He was sick of living with a woman who barely glanced at him, who only spoke to him to inquire whether he wanted fresh coffee, or what he wanted for dinner.

He was sick of being treated like a guest in a house he'd briefly considered his home.

The day after his and Lowrie's fight, he'd tried to ask her to give him some time, but she'd shut him down, telling him quietly and proudly that their association was over, to please forget they'd slept together. She intended to keep her distance and treat him like the guest he was. He protested, but she just left the room. That became the pattern for every interaction they'd had since. He'd raise the subject, she'd look at him with blank eyes and leave the room.

He hadn't managed to finish one nonguest question in more than ten days. And he was done. He was tired of looking at Lowrie and wishing, desperate to wrap his arms around her and never let her go. He was tired of hearing her laugh with Rhan and wishing he could be part of the joke, sick of watching her, Rhan and Charlie walking on the beach and wishing he was part of her circle. Exhausted from lying in bed and physically restraining himself from going to her.

No, he had to stay away from her until he could give her what she and Rhan needed. Security, love and understanding...his loyalty and his life. Besides, he wanted to walk into a new phase of his life, hopefully with her and Rhan, carrying as little baggage as he could.

"You okay, Sutton?" asked Garrett, who was standing next to Kinga, his hands in the pockets of his suit.

Sutton shrugged and brushed a piece of lint off the sleeveless parka he wore over a black cashmere sweater. Jeans covered his legs and fell over his battered hiking boots. His half sisters, uncle and Garrett were all wearing corporate boring, but Sutton wanted Callum to underestimate him because, well, that would be fun.

"I'm not a fan of waiting," he replied and got an answering grimace in response. Neither, it seemed, was Garrett.

Emma, Garrett's mother, opened the door to Callum's study and frowned at them. "He's ready for you now. I'd like to remind you all that he's still recovering from a profoundly serious operation so make it quick and *don't* upset him."

Sutton raised his eyebrows at her directive. She sounded more like a wife than a personal assistant. Had he missed something along the way?

But, unfortunately, there was no chance of not upsetting Callum, Sutton thought as they trooped into the office, lining up in front of his desk like errant school children at the principal's desk.

Callum, tapping on his keyboard, didn't bother to acknowledge them. After a few minutes, Sutton, who wanted to get this over with so he could move on to winning Lowrie back—he was sick of their cold war—rapped his knuckles on Callum's vast, antique wooden desk.

Callum sighed and finally leaned back in his chair, pushing his fingertips together. "Who are you?" he asked Sutton, forgetting that they'd met before.

"I am Benjamin's son, Sutton Marchant," Sutton replied. Certain Callum's heart could handle it, he dropped another conversational grenade. "And I own a quarter share of Ryder International."

Color rushed into, and out of, Callum's face, but his eyes remained steady and as cold as ice. He took a moment to speak, and when he did, his voice was deep and steady. "Name your price."

Sutton lifted his eyebrows. "For the shares?"

"Of course, for the shares," Callum retorted. "What else?"

Sutton spread his hands. "No 'welcome to the family'? No 'where did you come from?' Nothing?"

"The shares," Callum said through gritted teeth. "Name your price and I'll arrange for payment."

Sutton jammed his hands into the pockets of his parka and rocked on his heels. "Even if I wanted to sell you the shares, and I don't—I can't."

"Why not?" Callum demanded, his face mottled with fury. Sutton doubted he'd have a heart attack, but was starting to think that Callum exploding was a distinct possibility.

"The terms of Benjamin's will forbid it. He specifically stated that I could not sell to you."

"I… What… You…"

James sat down in one of the two chairs opposite Callum and looked across to Emma, who was standing next to Callum, her hand on his shoulder. "I'd like notes of this meeting, Emma."

Emma narrowed her eyes at him and shook her head. "Callum is my boss, not you."

"Mom, this isn't the time to be difficult, but this will do," Garrett said, removing his phone from the inner pocket of his jacket. He laid it on the edge of Callum's desk and Sutton saw it was recording their conversation. Like a lawyer's deposition, Garrett explained who was present and recited the date and time. He placed his hand on James's shoulders and squeezed, silently encouraging his father.

"Callum," James said, looking the Ryder-White patriarch in the eye. "As you know, a Ryder International board meeting is scheduled for tomorrow night."

"I know, I'm working on the agenda," Callum retorted.

"We've already set the agenda, Callum, and I will be chairing that meeting," James told him, his voice steady and uncompromising.

Talking over Callum's splutters, James continued. "The five of us have decided how Ryder International will be run going forward and you are no longer part of that equation. In fact, we would like you to tell the world that, following your heart attack, you have retired and will be resigning from Ryder International, as CEO and as chairman of the board."

Callum's bright blue eyes narrowed. "That will never happen. This is my company, my legacy. And who will run the company? *You?*"

James nodded. "Absolutely me. But, unlike you, I am not an egotistical ass and I am happy to take advice and support and direction from my son, my daughters and my nephew. I will be the face of the company, but they will very much be part of Ryder International going forward."

"I will fight you on this! I will wipe the floor with all of you and you will be ruined by the time I am done with you!"

It was a threat they'd expected and it didn't scare any of them. Sutton and Garrett shrugged, Kinga and Tinsley looked stoic and James smiled. It was his son's smile that pushed Callum to his feet. "Get out of my office! All of you! Emma, call my lawyer."

"That's your prerogative." James didn't move except to take out a piece of paper from his jacket pocket. "Before you do that, there is one more thing you should know, Callum."

Callum looked down at the paper, frowning. "What is that?"

James tapped his finger on the envelope. "None of us could work out why it took so long to get our DNA results back from the genealogy site WhoAreYou. We should've had them back ages ago and last week, when I phoned to inquire, I was given the runaround, a million and one excuses. I eventually threw my weight around—I learned to do that from you—and reached the CEO.

"He told me that he would rerun them immediately and that we'd have our results the very next day. I asked him to run Garrett's and Sutton's DNA as well, anticipating the legal challenges you might throw our way. I didn't want any queries about bloodlines to cause a holdup in the legal fight I knew you'd embark on."

Callum's eyes darted between the paper and James's face, excitement brimming in those depths. Excitement or madness? Sutton couldn't tell. "I presume there were many matches between us and the Delaware cousins, and the Boston Ryder-Whites? Where do we come from, originally?"

Sutton exchanged a puzzled glance with Garrett. It seemed to him that Callum had forgotten that they were trying to oust him from the company. All his attention was on his ancestry.

"What other connections did they find? Let me see!"

James sent Kinga, then Tinsley a should-I-be-doing-this? look and Kinga placed her hand on his, squeezing.

"If we don't tell him, Dad, he will just rerun the tests himself and find out, anyway. Just tell him. Quick and clean," Kinga told James, and Tinsley nodded her agreement.

James nodded, swallowed and spoke again. "The thing is, Callum, me, Kinga, Tinsley and Garrett do *not* carry the Ryder-White genes. Sutton, through Benjamin, does."

Callum dropped into his seat, seemingly smaller than he was when he'd stood up a few minutes ago. "What are you saying?"

"Your mom was either pregnant when she married your father or had an affair when she was married to him because the man you thought was your father, James Callum Ryder-White, isn't."

"Maybe Benjamin wasn't his son, did you think about that?" Callum shouted.

"We did consider that, but Sutton is related to the other Ryder-Whites, Callum, and you aren't." James stood up, buttoned his jacket and made eye contact with each of them before looking at his father. "The thing is, Callum, we don't care about DNA, about what some test says or who populates our family tree. We're a family, by choice, not by blood. We choose each other.

"Don't fight us, Callum, you'll lose. Your choice is either to retire, resign and remain part of our rag-tag, non–blue blood family or die a lonely, resentful old man, fighting a legal battle he will not win and dealing with the world knowing that you aren't, by blood, a Ryder-White," James continued.

"You're blackmailing me?" Callum demanded.

James shrugged. "*Blackmail* is an ugly word. Think of it as us giving you a reason to retire gracefully. You have until tomorrow morning to decide."

James inclined his head and moved toward the door. They followed him out.

Sutton looked at James's back and realized there was a new head of the Ryder-White family. They were being led by a good man, a decent man.

Yeah, he could maybe hang around this family a little longer.

Lowrie wasn't sure how much longer she could live with Sutton without losing it. She wasn't sleeping, couldn't concentrate and was less patient with Rhan than usual.

But what she was doing, surprisingly, was painting. She was using oils and color to paint out her frustration and sadness, creating vibrant, messy works that were technically useless but full of passion and anger and desperation.

Standing on the veranda in the weak sunshine, she nibbled the end of her paintbrush and looked at a half-dead vase of peonies. The flowers were a metaphor for how she felt—droopy, low on energy, washed out.

She missed Sutton, missed sleeping in his arms, his quirky smile, his deep voice and God, she missed his blunt way of talking and his strength, mental and physical. She missed their conversations, the rumble of his laughter, the way she sometimes caught him looking at Rhan, wonder and fear on his face.

Her heart felt heavy, her soul full of stones. She'd told herself not to fall in love but she hadn't listened. And yeah, she did love Sutton, in ways she'd never loved Kyle or Rex, in ways that were unexpected and delightful and heartbreaking.

Lowrie jabbed her brush at the canvas, scowling. Well, she'd fallen in love with him so she could damn well fall out of love with him. And yeah, that was a good idea because his reservation was almost at an end and it was time to start taking in normal guests.

Returning to life as she knew it.

Lowrie turned at footsteps and smiled at her Paddy, walking toward her carrying a neatly wrapped brown paper parcel under his arm. He'd returned from San Diego a few days ago and apart from shaking his head at overhearing a biting conversation between her and Sutton, hadn't commented on their frosty relationship.

She wasn't expecting his silence to last.

"What do you have there?" Lowrie asked, nodding at the packet.

"Feels like a frame," Paddy told her. "It came with a thick envelope embellished with the fancy logo of your Manhattan lawyers."

Right, she'd been expecting the delivery but was surprised it had all happened so quickly. Amazing what you could accomplish with the right incentive, Lowrie thought.

"Are you going to tell me what's going on?" Paddy demanded.

Lowrie shook her head. "No, not now." Maybe one day but today she was feeling a little too raw.

"Fair enough," Paddy replied. He angled his head. "Had a walk-in, looking for a room. He's in the front lounge."

She frowned at him. "We're still closed, Paddy, you know that. Couldn't you have sent him on his way?"

Paddy shrugged. "You're the manager, so manage. Where's Rhan?"

"With Jo," Lowrie said, wiping her paint-streaked hands on a rag. She took her parcel into the house, shaking her head. Men! They could occasionally be as useless as a glass hammer.

Lowrie stomped to the living room, saw the outline of a shadowed figure by the window and spoke before waiting for her eyes to adjust, trying to be cheerful. "Hi there. Sorry, the inn is temporarily closed and we're not taking additional— Sutton? What the hell?"

He stepped away from the window and her heart went into free fall. He was so good-looking, so masculine, the only man she could imagine in her life.

But she was just a side benefit.

Lowrie lifted her free hand. "Sorry, mistake. Paddy said a guest walked in looking for a room." She turned to leave but his low voice stopped her.

"He wasn't wrong. I *am* looking for a room."

She glared at him. "Well, then you're shit out of luck because I wouldn't rent you a bucket if your boat was sinking." She placed the painting on the seat of the nearest chair and shook her head. "Go back to England, Sutton, and let's all go back to normal, okay?"

"Not okay," Sutton replied. "Nothing is okay anymore. Or normal."

"Can't help you with that," Lowrie said, aiming for flippant and not hitting the mark. God, she was tired. Tired of feeling miserable and heartsore. "I've got to go, Rhan is—"

"Rhan is with Jojo and I bribed Paddy to get you in here and then to give us some privacy."

Lowrie scowled and leaned her shoulder into the doorframe. "Why? To say goodbye? It's easy, one word... 'Bye.'"

Sutton had the balls to smile at her. "I'm not leaving, Low, not until you and I have had a proper chat, an old-fashioned heart-to-heart."

Lowrie snorted. "You? Having a heart-to-heart? *Sure.*"

"I'll admit I'm a useless talker for a writer, but we *are* going to talk, Lowrie, so sit your pretty ass down."

Her spine snapped at his command and she was about to stomp away when he spoke again. "Please, Lowrie. Let me talk and then if you still want me to go, I will, no questions asked."

She pushed her fingertips into the skin of her forehead and cheekbones, knowing that Sutton was stubborn enough to follow her around until she let him say his piece. It was easier to just let him speak and get it done.

God, it hurt.

Sighing loudly, she turned and met his eyes. "Speak. Make it fast."

Relief jumped into his eyes and he asked her to sit down but she refused. Nodding, Sutton took a moment to gather his thoughts before telling her about his father, that he was, by birth, a Ryder-White and the only reason he wanted Benjamin's money was to fund his parents' charity—a home for orphans—back in the UK. He told her that Callum Ryder-White had resigned from Ryder International, that James was the new CEO and chairman of the board and that Sutton, Kinga, Tinsley and Garrett Kaye would be James's advisors. That his parents charity would be, from this point onward, funded by the Ryder Foundation and the profits he earned from Ryder International would be split between the two foundations.

"My birth mother runs the foundation and we came to an agreement."

Reeling under a deluge of information, Lowrie held up her hand. "You met her?"

Sutton jammed his hands into the back pockets of his jeans and rocked on his heels. "Yes."

"And?" Lowrie demanded, unable to stop the questions tumbling from her lips. "How did that feel? Was it weird? Are you going to spend time with her?"

Sutton's eyes, when they met hers, reflected his confusion. "She was young, very spoiled. Benjamin hadn't yet accepted the truth about his sexuality and shortly after their affair ended, he met Carlo, your uncle, and fell completely in love, according to Paddy. Penelope tried to tell Benjamin about me but he refused to listen. He didn't want her, or any other woman, tainting what he had with Carlo."

Lowrie gasped. Penelope? "As in Penelope Ryder-White?"

He nodded. "Fantastical, right?"

"I had a long talk with Paddy and you were right—he did know Ben and knew a lot about his and Carlo's relationship, but nothing about the trust and the shares," Sutton continued. "Ben and Carlo lived here, together, for a year, maybe a little more. They were, by all accounts, blissful."

Yeah, she was happy for them but she was more concerned about the man she loved and how he felt meeting his birth mother. "We were talking about how *you* feel about Penelope, Sutt."

He met her eyes again. "I'm not sure. Neither of us knows what to feel or how to deal with each other so we're kind of in a holding pattern. But I don't think I'm ever going to be able to call her Mom, or feel like she is my mother, if that's what you're asking."

"Of course you won't because you had a mom and Penelope can't take her place. Just like Ben can't take your dad's. You're a Marchant, not a Ryder-White."

Sutton started to smile, and it just grew bigger and bigger. "God, I love you."

The words came out of nowhere and were a bucket of icy water. Her eyes filled with tears and she stared down at the Persian carpet. "That's cruel, Sutton."

She heard him walking to her, felt his palm cradling her cheek, his knuckle lifting her chin. She forced herself to meet his surprisingly tender eyes. "I do love you, Lowrie. I will keep saying it until you believe me."

"But…" She waved her hands in the air. "But I'm a diversion, remember? A way to pass your time?"

He nodded and her heart sank. "You are and you will be because I intend to spend the rest of my life passing my time with you. And Rhan."

Uh…

"Look, I'm not sure where we're going to live, here or in the UK, or, I imagine, splitting our time between both, but wherever you and Rhan are is where I want to be."

He was going too fast—she couldn't keep up. "You want to be with *me*?"

"And Rhan."

She shook her head, not understanding. "You don't want kids, Sutton, neither do you want a relationship. You said that."

Sutton ran his hand down her arm, regret flickering in his eyes. "I said a lot of stupid stuff, Lowrie, all of which I regret. Let me make this clear… I want a relationship with you. I want to be Rhan's father. I want more kids. But only with you."

Lowrie, needing something to hold on to—her knees were definitely liquifying—gripped his sweatshirt in her fists and twisted the fabric around her hands. "I don't know what to say, Sutton."

Her heart felt like it was about to leave her mouth

and her stomach felt like it had dropped to her toes. Her world was inside out and upside down, but in a good way, in the *best* way.

"Say you love me. Or if you don't, tell me you think you can love me…"

She met his eyes, saw the vulnerability in those depths and bit down on her bottom lip at seeing him exposed, brave and open to rejection.

"Tell me you want to spend your life with me, making books and babies and paintings. Making me happy." His thumb skated along her cheekbone, sending sparkles of excitement dancing along her skin. "Because I sure as hell intend to make you happy, Lowrie."

Lowrie loosened her grip on his sweatshirt and it took all her courage to step away from him. Glancing around, she tried to reorientate herself, surprised to see that the furniture was still where it had always been, that the sun hadn't turned into a ball of sparkly colored diamonds and that the sea still pounded the rocks and the beach. Shouldn't the world have changed? At least a little?

Reaching for Sutton's hand, she tugged him over to the chair and gestured to the professionally wrapped parcel she'd received from her lawyer. "That's for you."

Sutton handed her a little frown. "I'm giving you my heart and you're giving me a… What is that? A painting? This doesn't bode well."

She placed a hand on his arm and squeezed. "Open it, Sutton."

Sutton frowned again but bent down to rip the paper off the frame. "Did you frame the painting you did while we had sex? I'm warning you, if that painting goes with me, so do you."

"Open it, darling."

It was the *darling* that did it and Sutton ripped away the paper to look down at the painting, his mouth falling open with astonishment. "It's Cordyn's *Darkness Before the Dawn*." He stood up, his eyes darting between her and the painting. "This is an expensive painting, Low. Why do you have it?"

She smiled, her eyes a little blurry. "I knew that I needed to move on from my past, from what my mom and Kyle did, from what Rex did, or didn't do. I told my mom and Kyle, through my lawyers, that I would settle, go away, if my mother gifted me that painting in lieu of what they owed me."

She released a small smile. "Jojo, as you can imagine, pitched a fit. She said I deserved millions, not a painting by some artist she'd never heard of."

"I happen to agree but we'll discuss that later." Sutton looked at her, his eyes intense. "Why this painting, sweetheart?"

She sniffed and dashed away a tear with the back of her hand. "Because it belongs with you, with the others you own. But mostly because I wanted something of mine to go with you when you left."

Sutton took her hand and rubbed his thumb across the ring finger of her left hand. "I'd far prefer it if we *all* stayed, or all left. You, me, Rhan, the painting, the other painting..."

Lowrie lifted her hand to trail her fingers down his cheek. "Are you sure?"

"Never been more certain of anything in my life. I'll love you, Lowrie. I'll love Rhan. I'll love him as much, maybe more, than any other kids we have. I know that now."

"I know that, too, Sutt. You wouldn't have it any other way. You just needed time to realize it," Lowrie told him, curling her hand around the back of his neck, and pushing her breasts into his chest.

"Okay," she murmured, standing on her toes to whisper the words against his lips. "Let's do this."

"Do what, darling?"

"Love each other, Sutton. Here, there, everywhere."

Epilogue

Lowrie sat, with Sutton, at the head of the long, exquisitely decorated twenty-five-seat table and looked up through the branches of the ancient woodland trees at the velvety, cloudless sky. Organizing an outdoor reception in the United Kingdom was a risk, but this small wood bordering Marchant House was a magical spot, full of history and mystery. Lanterns, candles, fairy lights and flowers—peonies, roses and camellias—added to the *Midsummer Night's Dream* theme and she wanted their special guests—friends who were family and family who were friends—to experience the magic of this spot where Sutton proposed just a few months ago.

Lowrie glanced down at her stunning engagement ring—sixteen diamonds surrounding a whopping rare blue, oval diamond—still unable to believe that she was now Sutton's wife, that her son would soon become a Marchant and that she had more family, and friends, than she knew what to do with.

Sutton, dressed in a tuxedo and open neck shirt, turned to face her and managed, somehow, to pull Rhan from her lap while dropping a hot kiss on her lips. He pulled back and smiled at her, his eyes tender. "You're looking a bit shell-shocked, my darling. Are you okay?"

Lowrie placed her hand on Rhan's chubby knee and looked up into her husband's gorgeous face. "I feel like I am having a bit of an out-of-body experience, to be honest. I can't believe this is my life."

He tipped his head to the side. "So you're happy then?"

Sutton adored her and her son, was a fantastic lover and her best friend. Happy didn't come close to describing her level of euphoria. She held her thumb and index finger an inch apart and grinned at him. "Maybe just a little," she teased.

Rhan pushed his hands against Sutton's chest in a bid to escape his grip and Sutton lowered him to the floor. He immediately toddled off on chubby legs, gleefully evading adults who wanted to scoop him up for a cuddle.

Sutton draped his arm across her lap and held her opposite thigh in his big hand. She rested her head on his shoulder and looked down the table at the laughing, happy crowd.

Jojo, who'd walked her up the aisle earlier, sat next to James and Penelope Ryder-White. Paddy was regaling Garrett and Cody with one of his tales, and Isabel was deep in conversation with Griff. Despite receiving an invitation, Callum was absent from the festivities, as were her parents.

Their choice…

Sutton dropped a kiss on her head before leaning back and looking at their ragtag family. He released a huge sigh when he saw Kinga, Tinsley, Thea and Jules huddled together, deep in conversation. "Look at them, I am sure they are planning world domination. Three sisters, Low, three!"

Lowrie laughed, not fooled by his mournful tone. He adored his sisters, and Jules, but Thea, naturally, would always be his favorite. She leaned back, crossed her legs and placed her elbow on the table, her chin in the palm of her hand.

"They are probably bouncing around ideas for the Ryder-White Christmas Ball," Lowrie told him. The ball would be smaller than the Valentine's Day one, though no less luxurious and it would take place in the ballroom of Marchant House a few days before Christmas. "I can't wait to dance with you under the mistletoe, Sutt."

Sutton stood up and held out his hand. Lowrie stood up and turned at the gentle sound of a strumming guitar. She looked around to see Griff leaning against a majestic oak, a guitar in his hands and a smile on his handsome face.

Sutton wrapped his arm around her waist. "Dance with me now, Low?"

Griff's rich voice filled the forest and Lowrie nodded. Of course she would...

Because in his arms, in his life, was the only place she wanted to be.

* * * * *

Don't miss any of
Dynasties: DNA Dilemma from Joss Wood!

WE HOPE YOU ENJOYED
THIS BOOK FROM

HARLEQUIN
DESIRE

*Luxury, scandal, desire—welcome to
the lives of the American elite.*

Be transported to the worlds of oil barons, family dynasties,
moguls and celebrities. Get ready for juicy plot twists,
delicious sensuality and intriguing scandal.

6 NEW BOOKS AVAILABLE EVERY MONTH!

#2881 ON OPPOSITE SIDES
Texas Cattleman's Club: Ranchers and Rivals
by Cat Schield
Determined to save her family ranch, Chelsea Grandin launches a daring scheme to seduce Nolan Thurston to discover his family's plans—and he does the same. Although they suspect they're using one another, their schemes disintegrate as attraction takes over...

#2882 ONE COLORADO NIGHT
Return to Catamount • by Joanne Rock
Cutting ties with her family, developer Jessamyn Barclay returns to the ranch to make peace, not expecting to see her ex, Ryder Wakefield. When one hot night changes everything, will they reconnect for their baby's sake or will a secret from the past ruin everything?

#2883 AFTER HOURS TEMPTATION
404 Sound • by Kianna Alexander
Focused on finishing an upcoming album, sound engineer Teagan Woodson and guitarist Maxton McCoy struggle to keep things professional as their attraction grows. But agreeing to "just a fling" may lead to *everything* around them falling apart...

#2884 WHEN THE LIGHTS GO OUT...
Angel's Share • by Jules Bennett
A blackout at her distillery leaves straitlaced Elise Hawthorne in the dark with her potential new client, restaurateur Antonio Rodriguez. One kiss leads to more, but everything is on the line when the lights come back on...

#2885 AN OFFER FROM MR. WRONG
Cress Brothers • by Niobia Bryant
Desperately needing a buffer between him and his newly discovered family, chef and reluctant heir Lincoln Cress turns to the one person who's all wrong for him—the PI who uncovered this information, Bobbie Barnett. But this fake relationship reveals very real desire...

#2886 HOW TO FAKE A WEDDING DATE
Little Black Book of Secrets • by Karen Booth
Infamous for canceling her million-dollar nuptials, Alexandra Gold is having a *little* trouble finding a date to the wedding of the season. Enter her brother's best friend, architect Ryder Carson. He's off-limits, so he's *safe*—except for the undeniable sparks between them!

*Attorney Alexandra Lattimore isn't looking for love.
She's home to help her family—and escape problems
at work. But sparks with former rival Jackson Strom
are too hot to resist. Will her secrets keep them from
rewriting their past?*

Read on for a sneak peek at
Rivalry at Play
by Nadine Gonzalez.

"Mornin'," Jackson said, as jovial at 6:00 a.m. as he was at noon.
He loaded Alexa's bag into the trunk and held open the passenger
door for her. "Let's get out of here."

Alexa hesitated. Within the blink of an eye, she'd slipped back
in time. She was seventeen and Jackson was her prom date, holding
open the door to a tacky rental limo. There he was, the object of her
every teenage dream. She went over and touched him, just to make
sure he was real.

"Are you okay?" he asked.

"No," she said. "I was thinking… If things were different back
in high school—"

"Different how?"

"If I were nicer."

"Nicer?"

"Or just plain nice," she said. "Do you think you might have
asked me to prom or homecoming or whatever?"

Jackson went still, but something moved in his eyes. Alexa
panicked. What was she doing stirring things up at dawn?

"Forget it!" She backed away from him. "I don't know why I

said that. It's early and I haven't had coffee. Do you mind stopping for coffee along the way?"

He reached out and caught her by the waist. He pulled her close. The air between them was charged. "I didn't want *nice*. I wanted Alexandra Lattimore, the one girl who was anything but nice and who ran circles around me."

"Why didn't you say anything?"

"I was scared."

"You thought I'd reject you?"

"If I had asked you to prom or whatever, would you have said yes?"

"I don't know," she admitted. "Maybe not…or I could have changed my mind. Only it would have been too late. You would have found yourself a less complicated date."

"And end up having a forgettable night?"

"That's not so bad," she said. "I would have ended up hating myself."

Alexa wanted to be that person he'd imagined, imperious and unimpressed by her peers or her surroundings, but she wasn't. She never had been. She'd lived her whole life in a self-protective mode, rejecting others before they could reject or dismiss her. She now saw it for what it was: a coward's device.

His hand fell from her waist. He stepped back and held open the car door even wider. "Aren't you happy we're not those foolish kids anymore?"

Alexa leaned forward and kissed him lightly on the lips. "You have no idea," she whispered and slid into the waiting seat.

Don't miss what happens next in…
Rivalry at Play by Nadine Gonzalez,
the next book in the Texas Cattleman's Club:
Ranchers and Rivals series!

Available July 2022 wherever
Harlequin Desire books and ebooks are sold.

Harlequin.com

Get 4 FREE REWARDS!

We'll send you 2 FREE Books plus 2 FREE Mystery Gifts.

FREE
Value Over
$20

Both the **Harlequin® Desire** and **Harlequin Presents®** series feature compelling novels filled with passion, sensuality and intriguing scandals.

Welcome to Four Corners Ranch, Maisey Yates's newest miniseries, where the West is still wild…and when a cowboy needs a wife, he decides to find her the old-fashioned way!

Evelyn Moore can't believe she's agreed to uproot her city life to become Oregon cowboy and single dad Sawyer Garrett's mail-order bride. Her love for his tiny daughter is instant. Her feelings for Sawyer are…more complicated. Her gruff cowboy husband ignites a thrilling desire in her, but Sawyer is determined to keep their marriage all about the baby. But what happens if Evelyn wants it all?

The front door opened, and a man came out. He had on a black cowboy hat, and he was holding a baby. Those were the first two details she took in, but then there was… Well, there was the whole rest of him.

Evelyn could feel his eyes on her from some fifty feet away, could see the piercing blue color. His nose was straight and strong, as was his jaw. His lips were remarkable, and she didn't think she had ever really found lips on a man all that remarkable. He had the sort of symmetrical good looks that might make a man almost too pretty, but he was saved from that by a scar that edged through the corner of his mouth, creating a thick white line that disrupted the symmetry there. He was tall. Well over six feet, and broad.

And his arms were…

Good Lord.

He was wearing a short-sleeved black T-shirt, and he cradled the tiny baby in the crook of a massive bicep and forearm. He could easily lift bales of hay and throw them around. Hell, he could probably easily lift the truck and throw it around.

He was beautiful. Objectively, absolutely beautiful.

But there was something more than that. Because as he walked toward her, she felt like he was stealing increments of her breath, emptying her lungs. She'd seen handsome men before. She'd been around celebrities who were touted as the sexiest men on the planet.

But she had never felt anything quite like this.

Because this wasn't just about how he looked on the outside, though it was sheer masculine perfection; it was about what he did to her insides. Like he had taken the blood in her veins and replaced it with fire. And she could say with absolute honesty she had never once in all of her days wanted to grab a stranger and fling herself at him, and push them both into the nearest closet, bedroom, whatever, and…

Well, everything.

But she felt it, right then and there with him.

And there was something about the banked heat in his blue eyes that made her think he might feel exactly the same way.

And suddenly she was terrified of all the freedom. Giddy with it, which went right along with that joy/terror paradox from before.

She didn't know anyone here. She had come without anyone's permission or approval. She was just here. With this man. And there was nothing to stop them from…anything.

Except he was holding a baby and his sister was standing right to her left. But otherwise…

She really hoped that he was Sawyer. Because if he was Wolf, it was going to be awkward.

"Evelyn," he said. And goose bumps broke out over her arms. And she knew. Because he was the same man who had told her that she would be making him meat loaf whether she liked it or not.

And suddenly the reason it had felt distinctly sexual this time became clear.

"Yes," she responded.

"Sawyer," he said. "Sawyer Garrett." And then he absurdly took a step forward and held his hand out. To shake. And she was going to have to… touch him. Touch him and not melt into a puddle at his feet.

Find out what happens next in Evelyn and Sawyer's marriage deal in Unbridled Cowboy, *the unmissable first installment in Maisey Yates's new Four Corners Ranch miniseries.*

Don't miss Unbridled Cowboy *by New York Times bestselling author Maisey Yates, available May 2022 wherever HQN books and ebooks are sold.*

HQNBooks.com

PHMYEXP0522

**IF YOU ENJOYED THIS BOOK
WE THINK YOU WILL ALSO LOVE**

HARLEQUIN
PRESENTS

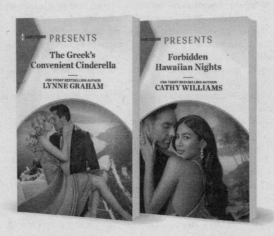

Escape to exotic locations where passion knows no bounds.

Welcome to the glamorous lives of royals and billionaires,
where passion knows no bounds. Be swept into a world
of luxury, wealth and exotic locations.

8 NEW BOOKS AVAILABLE EVERY MONTH!